JUST
FINE

Also by France Daigle

1953: Chronicle of a Birth Foretold
Real Life

France Daigle

Just

Fine

A novel

Translated by Robert Majzels

Anansi

Published in 1999 by
House of Anansi Press Limited
34 Lesmill Road
Toronto, ON M3B 2T6
Tel. (416) 445-3333
Fax (416) 445-5967
www.anansi.ca

Distributed in Canada by
General Distribution Services Inc.
325 Humber College Blvd.
Etobicoke, ON M9W 7C3
Tel. (416) 213-1919
Fax (416) 213-1917
Email Customer.Service@ccmailgw.genpub.com

First published in French as *Pas Pire*
in 1998 by Les Éditions d'Acadie.

03 02 01 00 99   1 2 3 4 5

CANADIAN CATALOGUING IN PUBLICATION DATA

Daigle, France
[Pas pire. Engish]
Just fine

Translation of: Pas pire.
ISBN 0-88784-639-4

I. Title.

PS8557.A423P3713 1999   C843'.54   C99-931349-5
PQ3919.2.D225P3713 1999-06-08

Printed and bound in Canada
Typeset by Brian Panhuyzen

*We acknowledge for their financial support of our publishing
program the Canada Council for the Arts, the Ontario Arts
Council, and the Government of Canada through the Book
Publishing Industry Development Program (BPIDP). This
book was made possible in part through the Canada Council's
Translation Grants Program.*

The author thanks the Canada Council for the Arts for its
support of the writing of this book.

JUST
FINE

1

Tale of a Step Dance

I

WINDY SUMMER IN DIEPPE. The sky is a solid white, that opaque white that, in winter, precedes a snowfall. But we're in summer, in mid-July, and the trees are covered in leaves, shaken and twisted by a wind that comes from everywhere at once, from high in the sky and from the ground, from the fields and from the city, from both ends of Acadia Avenue. This gusting wind has been blowing for days now, shuffling everything — not just the cards, but the rules of the game — to the point where we forget we're in summer, in Dieppe. Dozens of times I've recalled that summer when I separated myself from those who sit quietly at the dinner table.

I'm talking, of course, of Dieppe before the annexation of Saint-Anselme, and maybe even of Dieppe before Lakeburn. I'm talking of the old Dieppe, of central Dieppe, of the Sainte-Thérèse parish, with its Sainte-Thérèse Church beside Sainte-Thérèse School on Sainte-Thérèse Street. I'm talking about the Dieppe surrounded by fields and marshes that we burned every spring, fields of long grass through which slithered a few snakes and a river, the Petitcodiac, which seemed to cut right through our yards.

Between our houses and the river, there were more or less overgrown fields. Close to the houses there were lawns and yards where we played games with firmly established rules. Beyond the vegetable gardens and raspberry bushes and a few apple trees there was the true country, marshland covered in long grass, territory of invented games, games we mostly made up in the course of an afternoon, games full of dense grass that moaned when our pants and boots brushed against it.

Perhaps reflecting something of the nature and spirit of the scientists who study and describe them, deltas have some profoundly human characteristics: they start out in an embryonic state, emerge, and become rooted. When we chart the six ways deltas generally extend into the sea, the forms we call mouths do indeed resemble the shape of the human mouth. Young deltas are swaddled and flabby; eventually they lie down and thicken with age. Some have lobes, a forehead, arms, a hand, or fingers. We attribute ways of life to them; they experience breakups and accidents. If angered, some will go so far as to kill. Others quietly change beds, subdivide, or reproduce as subdeltas that, like children, are the offspring of the resources and power that formed them. Still others change paths according to circumstances, go over the top, take shortcuts, rid themselves of excess members. Deltas like to play: they love sand and slides and never tire of splashing about in ponds and basins. They race between their banks, sowing reeds and mangroves, sculpting flitches, and uncovering bogs. Since deltas are often more wide than deep, their meanders, swamps, and marshes regularly flood and overflow. Some overflows playfully open up additional beds each spring, setting off new processes, reversing the traditional exchange between fresh- and salt water, heedlessly disregarding the inextricable interpenetration of earth and water, and mischievously covering the world with a new layer of ambiguity.

❧

Madame Doucet, a very old woman in the neighbourhood, always had something for us when we brought her flowers. Our bouquets ranged from a lowly clump of dandelions plucked with little effort at her doorstep to more thoughtful arrangements of wild flowers that were, in those days, nameless. In exchange for whatever we had gathered that day, we invariably received a caramel, a slice of apple, a gingersnap, or a biscuit. It was a welcome snack near morning's end or in the afternoon when time dragged and there was nothing else to do. Even the boys occasionally indulged in this covert begging. We showed up at Madame Doucet's several times a week with our bouquets; that she never turned them down caused us to reflect on human nature, for we knew very well that our own mothers would never have played along. In the end, Madame Doucet's limitless patience and kindness so troubled our conscience that sooner or later, any self-respecting child quit the game of his or her own free will.

❧

Not every river is blessed with a delta. The fact that the Amazon and the Congo, the two biggest rivers in the world, don't have one proves that a delta requires very particular conditions. Indeed, coastal research by experts has revealed a host of nuances in these conditions. Scientists have distinguished simple deltas from complex deltas, bird's-foot deltas from bell-shaped and atrophied deltas. Their work also describes spring tides and neap tides, terrigenous sediments and flocculation, creeping soil and silting, turbid pluming, lagoons and mudflats, ravines and hummocks. These specialists have studied the age of deltas and have observed that the morphological evolution of many of them is comparable to that of a human lifetime. The differences among deltas, which depend upon weather conditions, the role of wind and vegetation, and the profound perturbations caused by human intervention, have been studied and the various stages in the fall of a river have been mapped. Shifts in riverbeds have also been recorded: the Huang He River, for example, has apparently changed its course and mouth twenty-six times in 3,000 years.

Not all children were obliged to be so inventive in order to satisfy their minor personal needs. In some houses, nickels for buying candies were doled out liberally. In others, there were candies in the candy dish all week long. In still others, when you expressed a need, you generally received some kind of response. But there were also houses where there was nothing to be done, where needs were never even expressed. Or those that were expressed were of a completely different nature. When visiting our friends, we slipped into the daily routine of their homes in the same way we got on a merry-go-round, trusting in the particular machinery of the place. Things happened in other kids' homes that were unthinkable in our own, sometimes for the better, sometimes for the worse. All this nourished our gaze. We picked up bits here and pieces there and gathered them together to invent a life. Our lives were composed of these things. Of useful things and useless things. Of things of certain value and things of no apparent value. Of things whose value remained to be discovered.

❧

A delta generally forms when the sea fails to redistribute over a wide area the sediment and particles transported by a large river. This transported material is gradually deposited at the mouth of the river, eventually creating small islands or accumulations that impede the water's free flow. To attain the sea, the river breaks up into several smaller rivers, the main branches of which appear to form the sides of an isosceles triangle when seen from the air. Hence the name *delta*, the fourth letter of the Greek alphabet, whose uppercase, Δ, has just such a triangular shape. The visible deltas, or those that present a relatively complex interpenetration of land and water, are the best known. But there are also subaqueous and tidal deltas, which are actually deltas in the process of forming and not considered true deltas. The only criterion for a delta relates to the incursion of land into sea. This incursion can be considerable: 30 kilometres in the case of the Danube, for example, and 140 kilometres in that of the Mississippi delta, which was long considered the biggest in the world. This honour now belongs to the Ganges-Brahmaputra delta. Even the multiplicity of branches is not a criterion for being a delta, although most deltas have many.

II

IT IS NEITHER FREE nor easy to be born. Buddhists say that it is more difficult for a human to be born than for a blind turtle wandering the depths of an ocean as vast as the universe to stick its head through a wooden ring floating on the water's surface. The turtle's feat is all the more unlikely because the ring is cast about by waves and the turtle rises to the surface only once every one hundred years.

Astrology, on the other hand, claims that every birth corresponds to a cosmic goal of the universe. This means that individuals who are born, or who enter into density, are the fruit of a will and a project, a double project really: perfecting themselves and serving the needs of the universe by contributing their unique abilities. The hour, day, year, and place of a person's birth determine the forces in play at that moment and throughout that life.

Astrology is a highly complex science. Some of its treatises are like prayers while others are poetry. Still others consist of extravagant mathematical tables and vectors. The purpose of these things is to show us that life has meaning and that each of us has a mission, a unique path to follow.

Astrology aspires to help people find their way so that they might fulfill their potential. One can ingest this information in small morning doses with one's breakfast or, from time to time, in direct consultation with a professional astrologer. The important thing is not to take astrology too seriously. It can work even if you take it with a grain of salt.

❀

In our case, the difficulty lay not so much in being born as in being born to something. Our first efforts toward that end were made at Acadia Elementary School, a grey, entirely square, two-story building across the street from the church. This was a school for grades one, two, and three. We began our apprenticeship under the watchful gaze of two Madame Cormiers, Madame LeBlanc, Mademoiselle Melanson, Mademoiselle Cyr, and Madame Dawson. At first, I put too many humps in my *m*s and *n*s. The teacher finally lost patience with me, which made me cry.

I'm talking about the Dieppe of my school friends Cyrilla LeBlanc, Gertrude Babin, Debbie Surette, Louise Duguay, Charline Léger, Gisèle Sonier, Alice Richard, Lucille Bourque, Thérèse Léger, and Florine Vautour; and the Dieppe of the older guys who hung out at the corner and had names like Titi, Tillote, Pouteau, Pep, Hum, Youma, Lope, Dunderhead, Hawkeye, and Blind Benny.

❀

Astrological signs are one thing, the houses of the governing stars are quite another. Each of the twelve astrological houses represents one of the major areas of human activity. In the progression from one house to another, an individual's abilities and aspirations evolve; from one to another, the physical and psychic body grows. The twelve houses, named for the place they occupy on the chart, represent a series of evolutionary stages. They deal with every aspect of an individual's development, from birth to death and beyond. As a whole, they constitute one of the five great components of the science of astrology. The other components deal with the actual signs of the zodiac, the planets, their aspects, and their transitions.

The chart of astrological houses looks like a pie with twelve slices. The first six houses are located beneath the horizontal axis and deal with the individual's growth in the material world, the material organization of life. Houses seven to twelve are found above the horizontal axis and deal with the development of consciousness. Each house relates in a particular way to its opposite house, so that we cannot study the forces in play in one without taking into account those in play in its opposite. Hence, the first house is associated with the seventh house, the second house with the eighth house, and so on. Each house also corresponds to the spirit of a sign in the zodiac. An individual whose heavenly chart shows a planetary concentration in a particular house will present characteristics corresponding to the sign associated with that house and to the sign associated with the time of that person's birth.

The firehouse siren wailed at nine o'clock every evening to remind children that it was time to go home. It also wailed when there was a fire. One day the nine o'clock siren did not sound. A part of our world disappeared. Later someone put up a wooden structure containing something that looked like a belfry on the roof of the little Acadia School.

We wondered if the addition was intended to replace the siren. We were told it was an alarm in case of war. I seem to remember the word nuclear. It was also suggested that we dig bomb shelters in our basements and store provisions down there, just in case. I mentally began to organize such a shelter in our basement, beside the shelves where we stored jams and a few canned goods.

⦿

Some of us passed Régis's store and the Palm Lunch restaurant on our way to school every day. The building that housed both these businesses and the barbershop was called the corner, because it was located at the crossroads of Dieppe's two main arteries, Acadia Avenue and Champlain Street. What made these streets main was probably that they led somewhere other than our friends' houses or the fields. Acadia Avenue led to Memramcook, Champlain Street to the airport.

Régis's was a grocery store with a butcher who sold meat, rounds of cheese, and headcheese. You could buy on credit there. We called it "marking it down." Régis brought out his notebook and marked down what we bought. Sometimes we paid on the spot. The store also offered a pretty fine selection of penny candies. All the other sweets — chips, sodas, chocolate bars, ice cream — cost five or ten cents. The Palm Lunch also had a candy counter. Often we took the time to compare the two displays before buying, hence the constant coming and going of children between both stores.

The Palm Lunch, whose name we rattled off without a clue as to its meaning, consisted of a long, slightly raised counter lined with spinning stools along one side and cupboards full of the sort of merchandise you'd find in any general store along the other side, next to the candy counter. The owner, Moody Shaban, would often cross from one side to the other to serve us himself. The pinball machines and the billiard table at the back of the restaurant made the Palm Lunch an ideal place to kill time. As it turned out, there were a lot of folks, especially guys older than us, with plenty of time to kill. There was also this one family that was very different from other families, if only because the parents and children often ate at the restaurant, sometimes individually, sometimes together, and sometimes at all hours. I envied them this free diet of hamburgers, hot dogs, french fries, and hot chicken sandwiches, but I wasn't too sure about the mother's dyed, teased hair. Because the palm of a hand was the only definition I knew for the English word palm, I thought the name of the restaurant referred to its fare, most of which you ate with your hands. It was only years later that I realized that the little green-and-red neon palm tree hanging in the window was more than a decoration. It was only years later that the reality, or the unreality, of that palm tree really sank in for me.

Another small store, the Nightingale, was located below the church, that is, at the bottom of the hill, beyond the church. Many of the kids at school lived down there on Orléans, Thibodeau, Gaspé, or Charles streets, to name a few. The people living on Gould Street practically had a variety store, Gould's, to themselves. Candies varied from one shop to another and when new stuff appeared in one store and not the others, it would spark jealousy among the children. The Nightingale became far more mysterious in my eyes when a teacher told us a nightingale was a bird.

@

Once a year, my mother had us make our own root beer. We were always happy to comply and, besides, the home-made brew was good for the family budget since it was cheaper than store-bought pop. We began by pouring a large amount of some liquid concoction into enormous cauldrons to simmer on the stove; then we bottled it all in tall beer bottles. The project was somewhat ambitious. We could never quite believe that so much root beer could come from such a small flask of extract purchased at the pharmacy. Once the bottles were filled, capped, and clean and smooth, we carried them, two at a time, one in each hand, up to the attic. There were probably three or four of us going back and forth to bring the root beer upstairs, where it was left to ripen until we brought it out on special occasions, such as Christmas, birthdays, the occasional Sunday, and, if there was any left, on summer days, when we went for picnics at Belliveau's Beach, our big plaid beach bag stuffed with towels and our willow basket containing a snack. I can still see the green, almost black, bottles wrapped in newspaper and lying one on top of another in the darkness of the attic. Here, already, was a work of art of sorts.

III

ON FIRE NIGHTS the world was full of energy. Our parents never tried to keep us at home on those nights, even though they knew we'd return blackened and full of smoke, our eyebrows singed, and our hair stiffened by the fumes. They would not deprive us of the magic that operated on those nights. It was as though they knew we were going out to do something important, essential even, like exercising our power. For that was indeed what was happening: whether we were spreading the fire or putting it out, opening or blocking the path of the flames, it was in our way, in each one's own way, of combining these two complementary acts that we measured our power and relished the crackling fire, the smell of the smoke, the spectacle of fire consuming a tuft of grass in a flash, the thrill of leaping through the flames, and the exuberant camaraderie of our friends and the others who took part in this sublime and savage ritual. We all enjoyed ourselves thoroughly, participating in an identical and spellbinding experience of the self.

It always began with a whispering back and forth at school. By suppertime, the entire neighbourhood was feverish and rife with murmured questions about the identity of the boy — what girl would have dared? — who would drop the first match. This single act of bravado unleashed a chain reaction; the scent of smoke spread and signalled the ultimate call to action. Soon after, the station siren and the flashing emergence of the fire trucks from the station confirmed that fire night had indeed been launched. Not a single field was spared. We got as close as we could to the houses where the firemen were stationed. In a way they were our accomplices, for they knew they could never stop what was a kind of collective release and so they were content to put out those flames that came too close to private property.

Late at night, after they had blackened all the fields in the interior, the fires moved quietly away from the town centre to burn freely in the swamps, advancing in long orange rays to their eventual extinction along roads, waterways, and other natural barriers. The next day, they often continued to smoke in the distance. It was sad to see all those burned fields around us in the light of day, but our good humour returned quickly enough when we remembered the marvellous energy of the night before. Besides, since we knew the fields would soon bloom again with fresh green grass, we convinced ourselves that we had helped renew nature. The sight of those charred fields never prevented the fiery delirium from taking hold of us again the following season.

Under the sign of Aries, the first astrological house is that of birth. There's an art to birth, a way to become and to grow that lends itself to a good life. This is evident at birth, by a baby's reaction to its environment, to its own body, and to that of others. The first house offers clues about the initial impression we make on the world and vice versa. It's the house of the individual prior to any external influence, of natural dispositions and tendencies, of heredity, of idiosyncrasies and style. It's the house of beginnings, of vital energy, of youth focusing on itself. It gives us an idea of how we present ourselves to the world, how we put ourselves forward. It's the house of what we do for ourselves and the place where we feel good when we are alone.

❧

Although we paid little notice to the river because it played no particular role (you could neither boat on nor swim or fish in it), the Petitcodiac nevertheless had a place in our lives. It was always there; large, brown, dammed, and inescapable, due to its colour, its wide low-water sludge marks, and its famous tidal bore. Yet we never cared much for this flat, slow-moving river, on the same level as everything else, hidden most of the time by its own high banks. It gave off no odour, ran without a sound, and paid no more attention to us than we did to it. But this quasi-absent river would take on surreal dimensions every time an Irving oil tanker came to replenish the enormous white reservoirs located at the river's bend, at the mouth of Hall's Creek. Just when we'd all but completely forgotten the river, a supertanker would appear without warning, looking for all the world as though it were floating on the marshes, sounding its foghorn only once it was well in sight. These sly arrivals have left an indelible mark on me. I remember wandering innocently in the fields, and glancing by chance over my shoulder only to see a giant oil tanker coming up behind me. To this day, when I go to my therapist, I can never decide whether to lie on my back or my stomach. I never know which, my spine or my chakras, needs more attention.

❀

There are many true deltas other than the one the Ganges and the Brahmaputra produce together in the Bay of Bengal and the one formed by the Mississippi, which is probably the most famous of them all. In Africa, the Niger River forms a vast delta where it plunges into the Atlantic Ocean at Port Harcourt and conceals an important interior delta, just as the Senegal River does. The Nile, the Rhône, and the Ebro form large deltas at their mouths in the Mediterranean. In Italy, the Po creates a great delta as it empties into the Adriatic and the Tiber creates a classic triangular delta as it flows into the Tyrrhenian Sea. Wide deltas appear too at the mouths of Europe's two longest rivers, the Volga and the Danube, which empty into the Caspian and Black seas, respectively. The Amu Darya, which runs through Turkmenistan and Uzbekistan, flows into the Aral Sea through an extremely broad delta, whereas the Lena River, in Siberia, creates a delta typical of cold, high-altitude regions and resembles our own Mackenzie delta. In hot, damp latitudes, such as in Asia, we find a great many of the world's largest deltas: the Godavari and Indus deltas in India, the Irrawaddy in Burma, and the Yangzi Jiang and Huang He in China. The Huang He, or Yellow River, carries huge quantities of alluvial deposits and produces annual floods which, because of the dense populations found in deltaic zones of humid tropical regions, become deadly. In North Vietnam, the Song Hong, or Red River, combines with the Song Da, or Black River, to form the Tonkin delta; in the South, the Mekong flows into the Cochin China delta. Some islands of Indonesia also have remarkable deltas, particularly at the mouth of the Mahakam in Borneo and the Solo in Java. In Tunisia, the Medjerda delta is a veritable museum of recent

geomorphology and is rich with lessons on the consequences of human intervention upon delta formations.

⊚

There were four vegetable gardens in the immediate neighbourhood of our family home. I can still see Madame Pinet,
Monsieur Bourgeois, Monsieur Gallant, and old Mina
Gauvin bent over their rows. For the most part, the neighbourhood vegetables that graced our table came from
the garden of Madame Pinet, who lived next door and
gave them to us. We also bought a few from Mina Gauvin,
mostly rhubarb and beans, but sometimes beets, carrots,
and cucumbers, too. Though we occasionally ate the
Bourgeois's and Gallants' vegetables, their gardens were
mainly beautiful landscape paintings evolving before our
eyes, through the windows of our kitchen.

⊚

I'm talking about the Dieppe of Bruegel the Elder, where
everyone erects their own interior monuments. I'm talking
about the Dieppe of the *Census at Bethlehem*, of its inhabitants flooding into the Green Crown Inn to pay their taxes
to the emperor. I'm talking about that little Flemish town
where people come from surrounding villages to exchange
the contents of their baskets, their demijohns, and their
crates of fowl. I'm talking about the peasant who slits a pig's
throat in plain view of everyone, about his wife who col-
lects its blood in a pan, and about the other animal awaiting
its turn, for there are suddenly many mouths to feed.
People, bent beneath their loads, are coming on foot across
frozen rivers; others have been here for some time. They've

arranged their barrel-shaped wagons for all to see, filled them with grain or wine, and now they're discussing, negotiating, arguing, sharing news. I'm talking about the chickens pecking at the ground at the feet of the artisan who's in front of the inn making and selling his chairs, three-legged straw seats also used as sleds by parents to pull their kids along the frozen river. I'm talking about a woman sweeping snow, a man lacing up his skates, children having fun spinning tops or tussling on the ice. Soldiers have gathered in front of one of the many buildings; nearby, a small crowd has collected around a fire, probably seeking its warmth. Maybe they're roasting wheat. Elsewhere, a few people are seated in the trunk of a not-quite-dead tree converted to receive other tired travellers. Here and there, people are pushing, pulling, taking care of business, building a cabin, carrying wood. In the courtyard of a small cottage, a peasant woman is bent over her cabbages, half-buried in the snow. There's a dog and several crows. Carrying a long saw on his shoulder, Joseph leads the donkey on which Mary sits, pregnant with Jesus. A bullock accompanies them. They are as much a part of this sixteenth-century winter landscape as the others, and are about to relive the drama of Christianity. Two individuals are also arriving, carrying objects that resemble the gifts of the Magi. They walk by a child seated on a sled who propels himself forward with small poles he thrusts into the ice. In the centre of the painting, an abandoned wheel stands straight up, frozen in the snow and ice. It has twelve spokes.

IV

GOOD YEAR OR BAD YEAR, Hard Time Gallant would buy all our wigglers. His store, the Marsh Canteen, was located at the other end of town, near the marsh that was fed by Hall's Creek and that separated the town of Dieppe from the city of Moncton. For a long time, his canteen was no more than a collection of shacks, only one of which could be heated and kept open in the winter. Short and fat and wearing thick glasses, Hard Time Gallant never spoke much, but he sold a bit of everything in his store, including produce and local foodstuffs such as oysters, salted and smoked fish, lard, Acadian poutines, and samphire greens; in short, food that wasn't particularly attractive to children.

With each spring thaw, Hard Time would sell fishing worms again and we would become his suppliers. When we needed money, we'd spend an hour or two digging, and then bring him a can containing a respectable number of lovely wigglers all tangled up together. Whether our can was large or small, and whether it contained worms that were fat or thin, shiny or earthy, Hard Time would take it in his hands, shake it slightly to make sure we hadn't padded it with too much dirt, and, glancing at us through his thick glasses, he'd pull a few coins from his pocket or the cash register. He rarely gave us less than ten cents, and sometimes he'd give us up to thirty-five or forty cents. There were those who dared to quibble over the price. Sometimes you got more or less than you expected. It was difficult to determine what had, on a particular day, played for or against you. Each time we went digging, we tried to take into account our previous experience, Hard Time's last look, his last gesture; but at no time did he ever refuse our worms. I have no idea if he managed to sell all the worms we brought him.

Under the sign of Libra, the seventh astrological house is the house of one-to-one relationships, whether marital or professional. Upon entering a house situated above the horizon, one passes from the private to the public, from night to day, from adolescence to adulthood. This passage prompts a search for partners to help accomplish or obtain together that which is beyond the grasp of one alone. This is the house of marriage and family, of contracts and clients, of minor lawsuits and adversaries. Here we learn to compromise, to deal with others and with the public. In the seventh house, we see ourselves through the eyes of others; thus, the importance of making the right impression, of presenting ourselves in a good light, a light that does us justice but does not blind others. Hence this house's emphasis on moderation and balance, harmony and prudence.

France Daigle

I don't recall how old I was when I first read *The Diary of a Young Girl* by Anne Frank, but I remember very well that it plunged me into an incredible imaginary adventure in which I replaced the characters in the book with my own parents, brothers, and sisters. Unable to picture clearly in my mind the layout of the house where the four members of the Frank family and four of their Jewish acquaintances hid from the Nazis during the Second World War, I imagined the whole story taking place in our family's attic, a far smaller space than the three-floor annex in which at least five rooms had been modified to harbour the fugitives. And so, confined in a space as close as I could imagine, we moved, mostly on all fours in near total darkness, through tiny hallways bordered by trunks and cardboard boxes. A few slits let in the light in daytime and the cold in winter. There was no room for any furniture; at night we slept curled up most of the time because there was insufficient room for everyone to stretch out. Neighbours brought us food secretly and we tried not to be too hungry. We were very brave. Our parents were in charge, and we, the children, put our trust in them. For once, we managed to be truly reasonable. When conflicts arose we didn't allow them to fester. Each of us had to swallow his or her pride; it was the only way. The big difference, for me, was the cat. Its name was Kitty. In fact, Kitty is the name Anne Frank gave her diary, which she regarded as a confidante. The young writer rarely mentioned the annex cat, Mouschi, whose task it was to catch the rats that raided the food stocks at night. I turned Kitty into a real cat that I imagined walking and leaping with great agility here and there among the boxes of our cramped shelter. For my own comfort, I turned the two rats Kitty was charged with attacking into cowardly creatures that wouldn't dare come near so long as there was the slightest movement and, in our perilous hideout, there was always someone moving about.

I can't recall how old I was when I first read Anne Frank's *Diary*, but that book took me directly to Moody Shaban of the Palm Lunch, the first real-life Jew I ever knew. For months, if not years, I watched him to uncover what was particular about him, how he might differ from us non-Jews. Just that. Just an open gaze, a desire to understand.

I'm talking about the Dieppe of the Landing, of that disastrous expedition whose only positive outcome was the cautionary lesson it provided for future operations. Dieppe, August 1942: only perfect synchronization could have saved the gigantic amphibian assault from catastrophe — 237 warships of every sort and size travelling at different speeds, and 67 squadrons mobilized for the aerial attack. I'm talking about the importance of darkness, of surprise, and of a coordinated approach at the hour of the setting moon. I'm talking about yellow, blue, red, white, green, and orange beaches and of more than 6,000 men, a good number of whom knew they were going to their death. I'm talking about the fortress of Dieppe, the impenetrable ramparts erected by the Germans to counter any attack from the sea, the kilometres of barbed wire and the enormous concrete barriers mounted with rifles, machine-guns, and cannons of every kind. I'm talking about the deafening silence in the commander's cabin, far out at sea, as he waited for the troops to report their advance, not realizing the extent of the massacre, unaware that the Germans had made a priority of targeting communications equipment and its operators. I'm talking about the battle they couldn't chart on the enormous military strategy maps because key words were garbled in the few, confusing messages that did come through. I'm talking about thousands of men who failed even to set foot on land because the enemy's ferocious attack riddled the landing crafts and their human cargo with bullets, and left hundreds of men in the water and thousands more dead on the beach at the foot of the cliff. I'm talking about those who were able to desert before they could be captured by the Germans, made prisoners of war, and forced to endure the long agony of famine and humiliation. I'm talking about a boy on the outskirts of a village named Belleville-sur-Mer who helped the only truly victorious Allied troops that morning by providing them with information about German guns deployed in the village. I'm talking about an ordinary soldier, killed as he crossed an orchard. I'm talking about the guts of Dieppe, the stink of defeat, the hero complex, and the delirious workings of our strengths and weaknesses.

@

Of all the abstract concepts we were required to grasp, eternity was the one I found most difficult. Mainly because nothing we were offered in the way of a Heaven satisfied me. I could see no pleasure in floating endlessly on a cloud, and, besides, I knew it was impossible to do so. I had to imagine a more plausible paradise, one that was equally simple and just as monotonous. All I could come up with was a small dirt road, like the kind you find by the sea, a two-track path with a band of grass down the middle. I liked walking barefoot along such beaten paths because they were covered in a thin layer of very fine dirt, even finer than sand. I loved that almost-blond dirt; I loved to set my foot down in it and to lift my foot and let the tops of my toes trail just a little in it. That was all my imagination could muster as a simple Heaven. As for spending eternity there, I saw myself walking hand in hand with a beautiful Jesus all dressed in white, each of us in a track. To make our journey eternal, I projected a long curve in the road, so that its end was never in sight. Great concentration was required so as not to succumb to fatigue and boredom at the prospect of a walk that was likely to become tiring and dull. Because the company of Jesus did not exactly set my heart pounding.

Charles-Édouard Bernard, commonly known as Chuck Bernard, was Dieppe's first official biker. He earned his stripes in Toronto with the Satan's Choice gang and caused quite a stir when he returned one fine May day, decked out in his filthy clothes and on his equally demonic Harley-Davidson. Instantly a nervous feeling spread through town; it would last for weeks. People said he was capable of anything. Some even claimed that Chuck had been spotted in the parking lot of the Palm Lunch greasing his long black hair with motor oil from his Harley. Personally, I never saw him do it, but anything is possible.

V

IN THE FIRST DAYS of summer we were kept busy picking tiny wild strawberries in the big field just behind our house. At first, the heat and the sun were enough to lend excitement to this small excursion, buckets in hand, into the fields. But over days and years, the juice that reddened our fingers and the little gobs of spittle full of minuscule pale-green insects that stuck to our legs gradually caused us to lose interest. But strawberry picking was a prelude to picking blueberries, which grew farther from the house, near the racetrack. Blueberries were more fun to pick and they made a small, dry, pleasant sound when they fell into our bucket, glass bowl, or plastic container. The choice of receptacle was determined by a number of factors, an important one being that we liked to ride our bicycles to the patches and, though biking doubled the appeal of the outing, it also required a good deal of ingenuity to get home without spilling the tiny fruits of our labour.

@

Under the sign of Taurus, the second astrological house is the house of talents and personal resources, of emotions, and of the need to realize one's potential. It's the house of values and of one's own value. The house of spiritual talents and abilities, it is the house of the body, particularly of the muscles and the sense of touch, and of one's attitude toward material things: comfort, sensuality, personal freedom. The second house is also the house of aptitude for financial gain and management, but this appetite can also lead to eventual financial loss. This makes it also the house of personal debts, of a multiplicity or lack of revenues, and of one's perceived buying power and financial situation. Agriculture, banking, and the food industry occupy a large place within the house, along with a tendency toward generosity or selfishness. House of riches in so far as one is able to accept and enjoy them, the second house also represents our capacity to acquire power and to use it.

The child-king in his patch of blueberries, a condition which was more or less complex depending upon commercial considerations, mosquitoes, cigarettes, and the indulgence or strictness of parents. There was an existential side to blueberry picking, a slightly bluish tinge that was entirely absent from the picking of tiny strawberries, probably because we abandoned the strawberry field for the blueberry patch around the beginning of adolescence, when we were able to fully appreciate the advantages of picking that little, round, firm fruit. No more dilemmas over removing stalks: was it preferable to remove the strawberries' stalks as you went along or to wait until you got home? The blueberry was obviously preferred simply because it required no such additional and tedious handling. I should add that, for some reason perhaps related to their scarcity, the tiny strawberries seemed to be destined for our households only: it never occurred to us to sell them for a handful of change. Blueberries, on the other hand, were ideal for selling and we were free to split our harvest between home and the market: the first basket went toward a family pie and the second was sold to a neighbour or passer-by. The profits went directly into our pockets. The commercial aspect of blueberry picking made it more attractive to everyone, parents and children alike. It also justified straying farther and farther from home, since we had to get to the patches. As a result, blueberry picking occasionally turned into a cigarette orgy, during which we exhaled in a single breath our troubles, our idleness, and our dreams, all of them innocent and profound.

Of all archetypes — those primordial creatures that dwell within us — the hero is probably the most universal. A kind of tribal character caught up in a series of wild adventures in which all manner of strengths and weaknesses contend, the hero serves as a model for all those who despair. By his amazing survival, which he owes mostly to a series of resurrections, the hero encourages individuals in their personal quests and helps society develop a culture out of chaos. Both tasks seem huge and explain why heroes are often individuals who, like Hercules or Ulysses (the most famous heroes of classical mythology), must face a long journey.

Heroes are always born under miraculous circumstances and exhibit some unique superhuman strength very early on in life. But as great as their strength is, the tasks assigned to them are, for the most part, beyond measure. Moreover, once they have surmounted the innumerable obstacles given to them they risk falling prey to the machinations of jealous contemporaries or falling victim to their own pride. In the end, their struggles rarely achieve complete victory, as happiness is granted only to those who navigate wisely through the shoals, accept the advice of their protectors (heroes receive almost as much help as opposition in the course of their exploits), and draw strength from the destructive forces they face.

◎

When we wanted to explore beyond the fields behind our house, we set out for the woods behind Sainte-Thérèse School, where the path to the Three Streams began. You had to walk through a small forest for about a half mile to get to the First Stream. Just before getting there, you would come upon a small clearing of shorn grass from which several large rocks protruded. A few dozen feet farther was the stream with its almost-overgrown banks, on which you could sit and have a picnic. We would build a small fire and cook potatoes in the embers. Anyone could easily reach the First Stream; there was hardly any danger of getting lost. The path to the Second Stream was more overgrown, so that we could see very little on the way. I made it only once as far as the Second Stream. Because it was farther, almost as soon as we were there we had to think about getting back. The distance to and rumours about what went on at the Third Stream never inspired me to go there. When all is said and done, I was a First Stream girl, but I would have liked to have been alone more often at the stream, to splash about at will, to make a fire as I pleased, to catch a trout, or to watch for beavers. But the others who went there took none of this seriously. They talked loudly and teased each other endlessly before chasing, catching, and fighting or kissing one another on the mouth, depending upon the repulsion or attraction of the moment.

◎

Although Hercules accomplished many deeds, we remember him mainly for his physical strength and the twelve mighty labours, which he was obliged to undertake in order to purify himself of the murder of his children. Hercules was not a very disciplined student and had already killed his music and literature teacher, Linus, by striking him in a fit of rage with either a footstool or a lyre. He escaped punishment by pleading self-defence but his father, fearing more fits of madness, sent him to tend cattle in the countryside. Later, after he accidentally killed his children — was this the result of an evil spell cast on him by Hera? — Hercules wanted to kill himself but was convinced not to and given the twelve mighty labours as an opportunity to atone for his sins. In psychoanalysis, the twelve labours of Hercules symbolize the long and painful process of self-education needed to attain wisdom and serenity.

Most of the twelve labours involve the killing of animals, people, or evil monsters, but there were also times when Hercules was simply gallant, liberating worthy beings here and there. He could be helpful too. For example, he cleaned the Augean stables, where the dung of hundreds of animals had been collecting for decades, in one day. To do this, Hercules implemented the brilliant idea of diverting two rivers so that the waters would run through the stables. The fact that he demanded payment for his work does, however, cast a shadow on the legitimacy of this exploit and on our hero's altruism. Also worthy of note, some of the twelve labours were executed in Arcadia, an idealized place where people lived in harmony with nature and where song and music flourished. It was in Arcadia that Hercules confronted the birds of Lake Stymphalus, which were devouring the crops and killing travellers.

VI

AT TIMES, IT SEEMS as though I've completely forgotten to fly. As kids, when we were tired of playing in the field, we'd stop our berry picking, our games, everything, and simply lie down on our backs to watch the sky. Often, actually always, airplanes would be crisscrossing above, painting long stripes of white smoke. In the sun's reflection, the airplane sparkled as it advanced, oblivious to the world, oblivious to those of us below who had nothing better to do but to watch it pass. Lying there on my back, I became the pilot, I would become a pilot. Nothing seemed more marvellous. But no. Something happened. It's as though I forgot to fly. I became earthbound. I move along close to the ground, I no longer defy gravity. When I see birds in full flight, I'm fascinated, I vaguely remember something, a possibility, an attitude, an altitude, but that's as far as it gets. I've completely forgotten to fly. I no longer know how to fly. I unlearned it.

Under the sign of Scorpio, the eighth astrological house is the house of profound transformations, including death which, in its broadest sense, is a separation from that which is old. As well as being the house of dead things, such as antiques, archeology, numismatics, and philately, the eighth house pushes us through the great stages of decline and death in order to attain rebirth. It's the house of severe illness, of injuries and accidents, of adversaries and all obstacles we must overcome in order to take full possession of our destiny. It's also the house of every manner of assistance received from others and of every sort of financial transaction. We find here inheritances, bequests, wills, and the eventual advantages resulting from the death of others. It's the house of easy money, of income obtained with little effort, such as through annuities, licences, grants, copyrights, and commercial monopolies. Taxes, pensions, and life insurance are also on the inventory of this house, which invites us to go beyond the security we know toward the unknown of the self. For the eighth house is the house of spiritual renewal and mysteries, of sexual instinct as ability and emotional depth, of criminology, of the occult, and of the great beyond.

On Halloween nights, we raced over to the Babins' to get some taffy. Good taffy that was absolutely clear and hard like Madame Babin's had become rare. Even on Halloween, there wasn't enough to go around. Which is why, if you really wanted some, you wasted no time in getting to Beauséjour Street. The parallel streets of Sainte-Croix and Grand-Pré had some pretty special stuff to offer as well.

We must have lived a little too far from Madame Babin, because she was always just giving her last taffy away when our group arrived. On the sidewalk outside her door, the word passed along:

"There's no more . . ."

"No more taffy . . ."

This was stated in a sober, factual tone. It was fate in its most serious and elementary expression. After that, the sequence in which we went through the rest of the neighbourhood mattered little.

@

Like astrology and mythology, dreams can also enlighten without obliging us to act in any way. Some dreams, however, are more revealing, more engaging than others. For example, this dream I had on the beach one beautiful summer afternoon: I'm a baby again, my eyes are shut, I'm lying in my little hospital bed. I've just been born. Hands appear, begin to caress my body, massaging me all over. I am overcome by a feeling of warmth and happiness. I realize that I'm alive, and I am absolutely certain that, one day, I will walk.

And yet, I often have a completely opposite dream. In this dream, I feel a pain spreading in my legs until they can barely support me or carry me forward. The pain intensifies whenever I have to cover any given distance, to cross a street, for example. Then, because of the pain, I am unable to walk quickly, and I'm afraid I'll be hit by the car that is inevitably coming straight at me. The danger is always very real but I manage to escape every time. I keep going in spite of the pain and I manage, almost crawling, to reach a place where I'm safe, where I can sit and rest. It's not always a physical danger that compels me to move. Sometimes it's sheer stubbornness that drives me to go somewhere. Once, I had to climb a sloping alley to get to a convenience store owned by a Jewish family that was selling some rare specialty. No matter how bad the pain gets, it will not deter me from my objective. The pain itself seems to be the culmination of this recurring dream and I'm always surprised to wake up in a body that is not hurting. But the trace of this pain is never entirely wiped out of my mind.

@

Crossing the Dieppe intersection to get to the Esso service station, Chuck Bernard notices a crack in the asphalt, then another, and another. Suddenly, Chuck Bernard can see that the asphalt is full of cracks of different colours, which transform themselves quite naturally into a network of multicoloured threads floating on the surface of a stream. Chuck Bernard continues to cross the intersection on foot but, from his point of view, he's walking in a stream and pulling hundreds of multicoloured threads around his waist. The farther he goes, the harder the going becomes. At one point, he turns around and sees a large V dragging in the water behind him. He goes on but the threads have now tightened around his waist. Lowering his head, Chuck Bernard looks at his belly, sees that the threads have sliced through his body, that he's now cut in half at the waist. Chuck Bernard believes that everyone should take LSD once in their life, just to have a better idea of what reality conceals.

"I mean good LSD like the stuff we had back then."

@

The project was to write a book dealing very loosely and freely with the theme of space: physical space, mental space, and our ways of moving in them. Of being moved.

For space is not a strictly physical notion. It's not just an expanse, measurable or not, situated somewhere between the chaos of origins and the organized world we know. To exist legitimately, a space requires only one thing: that something move within it. It can be a proper physical space, according to the definition of three axes and six directions, or it can be psychic and represent the universe of potentialities. These two dimensions, one internal and the other external to the human being, confer on space a doubly incommensurable expanse. In both dimensions, there is a dilation toward infinity and a problem locating a centre.

It will take some time for the overall picture to emerge. Hence the symbol of the snail advancing slowly, carrying its house on its back, symbol of perpetual motion, symbol also of the pilgrim's voyage toward an internal centre. We can expect a number of digressions, paths that are more or less clear, more or less significant. Fiction writers are not the absolute masters of their works. For example, as I write these lines, the character, if one exists, remains an enigma. Perhaps this enigma will be resolved as we go along, but don't count on it. It might just be a Tentative Eventual Person who, in the beginning, could be called just TEP. In the feminine, Teppette, preceded by an *s*, Steppette, meaning in French, little hop, little step dance, little demonstration of agility, generally executed in space.

2

Therapy of Exposition

VII

WHEN I CAME HOME that day I found a message asking me to call the press attaché of the provincial inter-governmental affairs minister as soon as possible. I was surprised. I had no idea what he could possibly want to talk to me about. Politics was not something I had ever thought of getting involved in and I saw no reason to change my thinking on that score. This call from the minister's office, therefore, took on extraordinary proportions and I was driven to extravagant fantasizing. Suddenly, everything became possible, even opportunities I had never dared to imagine. Maybe a Québec author had expressed interest in my work and wanted to come work with me in Moncton as part of a cultural exchange between the two provinces. Better still, perhaps the director of *Bouillon de culture*, TV5's cultural magazine, had contacted the minister during a recent official visit to France, and begged him to send me to Paris to participate in the program. The host, Bernard Pivot, had insisted on it. He'd read my last book and found it very amusing. Immediately, my life began to flash before my eyes: Dieppe, Hard Time Gallant's Marsh Canteen, and the wigglers we dug up for a few nickels and dimes, the little, grey wooden school-house and Moody Shaban's Palm Lunch, the marsh in flames and the tufts of grass frozen in the ice of the bog, the tiny strawberries in the fields, the Three Streams, and Irving oil tankers on the Petitcodiac. I was prepared to tell all, they only had to ask. The words wanted nothing more than to come out. Life had perhaps never been told this way before. The questions would be sincere and interested and my answers would flow, clear and honest. There would be a feeling someone was being discovered. The germ of recognition, all of a sudden, after so many years. They would listen to me at last. It would be like a second birth, as important as or perhaps more important than the first.

@

When I got to Marie's, she was plucking a chicken to make a fricot. I gathered up my courage, because the smell of Acadian bouillon sometimes makes me nauseous and, unlike many of my compatriots, I find it increasingly diffi-cult to swoon over a bowl of fricot. In any case, the main thing to establish here is that I didn't turn back. Because, when you're agoraphobic, you often turn back, almost whenever you're unable to relax in the face of adversity. It's called avoidance.

In the beginning, Marie was no more than a good neigh-bour to me. It's only because of the children that she became a friend to whom I can tell anything. Well, almost anything. Her two kids are a handful, mainly because they're spoiled, and she knows it but that doesn't stop her from going right on spoiling them. I like people who trans-gress, who commit their mistakes consciously.

"Julien, pick up your stuff before someone falls over it and spills their poutines, or I'll mash you!"

It's also Marie's direct way of speaking that endeared her to me. I got a taste of it in the course of carrying out our respective parental duties. Nothing beats a sale of poutines in support of some extracurricular school activity to bring out all of your existential poison and make you wonder, really, what could possibly have possessed you to produce these little creatures who never stop squirming and writhing all around you — and all this, even if you do see some value in the activity in question. In this case, it was an exchange trip with students from Meune-sur-Saône.

"All the way over in France, eh! Well, aren't they lucky!"

Under the sign of Gemini, the third astrological house is the house of life's context. The house of brothers and sisters, of cousins and neighbours, people we don't choose but who nevertheless reflect our personal aspirations. It's the house of public places, of short trips, and of means of transportation. As the house of physical and social mobility, it pushes us to go toward others, to emerge from anonymity. The third house influences our ability to deal with the desire to ascend the social ladder, as well as the occupations and concerns that result from it. The third house is also the house of the mind's abilities: common sense and intelligence, innate talents, comprehension, the ability to grasp ideas and to deal with those around us, and the sense of belonging to a network, as opposed to living in solitude and stagnation. It's the house that enables us to envision how far we can go, both physically and psychologically. House of communication in all its forms, the third house is also that of writing.

It turned out to be the best (or, for me, the worst) case scenario. I confided in Marie that I was summoned to Paris to appear on the *Bouillon de culture* program. Of course, I had to explain to her what sort of bouillon it was and who Bernard Pivot was. In short, how glory itself had fallen so low as to turn its gaze on me.

"You mean it'll be like the old *Saturday Night Live* with Eddie Murphy, except without the sketches or the ads?"

I didn't dare admit that I'd never watched *Saturday Night Live*. "Something like that."

I could feel Marie doubting, for a fraction of a second, the attraction of such a program. But, as always, she abandoned herself to the throes of optimism and rejoiced in my success, confiding that she'd always known something exciting would happen to me. The bones of her stewed chicken lay in their grease a little longer than usual before she drained and tossed them into one of the six recycling bins — regular paper, newspaper, plastic, metal, glass, and organic waste — neatly aligned in the new post-overconsumption cupboard designed for our new society. Marie wanted to know when I was leaving, where I would stay, if I'd go alone, and what else I'd do over there. And that's when I was more or less obliged to make my confession.

❧

Upon entering the shop, I asked to be served in French. A proud and hardy Brayon appeared before me. I guessed he must be the owner of the muddy amphibian vehicle I'd seen in the parking lot. I was more or less certain I was dealing with one of those weathered francophones from the Madawaska region of New Brunswick who live for weekends spent exploring interminable forest paths in hopes of discovering a mountain, a new lake, or, with a bit of luck, a

moose in the mist. I know some of these people personally and, though I admire their penchant for wide open
spaces and faraway places, I must say I have my own good
reasons to forget they exist.

I was explaining to the salesman that I wanted to buy a
cellular phone but that I knew nothing about them. He
directed me to a shelf overflowing with various models,
each one more enticing than the next. I explained that I
wanted a small, light, portable phone. I was wavering
between a model you could plug into the car lighter and a
battery-operated, completely portable phone. Naturally, I
didn't want to pay more than necessary, especially not for a
host of features that were of no use to me.

The young salesman did his utmost to serve me. It was
more than I needed. Frankly, I would have preferred a few
minutes of silence to think quietly about which model and
features best suited my needs. The salesman continued to
bombard me, alternating between technical information
about which I understood practically nothing and questions
on the nature of my work and the use I intended to make of
the cellphone. I explained that, on the whole, I would make
very little use of it, that it was mostly to keep in contact with
people, my family, for example. This information didn't
seem to satisfy him. He asked a few more questions and, in
response to my somewhat evasive replies and in a tone that
betrayed his growing impatience, he said, "If I knew what
business you were in, I might be able to help you."

Poor man. He wanted so badly to be helpful that he
ended up being a pain. I didn't really feel like confiding in
him and telling him I was agoraphobic and couldn't bear
wide open spaces and that the phone was to call for help in
case I panicked. So I cut off the discussion and chose a
popular model, a decision that seemed to please him. While
he was filling out the plethora of forms, I eyed my new
phone uncertainly. I wasn't entirely sold on the idea of

acquiring this crutch but at least it would please my psychologist, who would see in it yet another sign of my will to be cured.

◎

Apart from the few close friends I had to inform, I rarely spoke about my "business." It's a fact that agoraphobes are absolutely ashamed of their neuroses. Irrational fears one has difficulty in understanding and accepting oneself are not exactly the sort of thing one enjoys sharing with others. Especially when one doesn't appear to have problems. As Marie exclaimed when I explained my situation, "You? But you've travelled all over the bloody place!"

Travelled is a big word for what I did. I was young and determined. I thought the new physical sensations were more or less normal, a consequence of being physically and psychologically separated from my childhood environment. I wanted so badly to forge ahead, not to be left behind, that I never realized that this thing I was feeling was fear. I continued along in spite of everything, in spite of myself, seeking calm here and there, and occasionally finding an oasis where things were okay, where there were kind people I could rely upon if ever the thing manifested itself, if my body and my head began to respond, if the thing erupted. For one of the big nuisances of agoraphobia is precisely the fear of finding yourself without the help of someone who understands or gives the impression of understanding what's happening and who knows how to react.

Even so, Marie was incredulous. She added, "Well, and what if you'd won the France-Acadia Prize last year, then? How were you planning to go over there to get it?"

I had to explain to Marie that, in fact, it had been a great relief not to have won the prize because I couldn't possibly imagine "going over to get it."

VIII

I WAS TAKING A RISK confiding in Marie. I was afraid of being told that things would work out fine if only I'd put my faith in God once and for all. Marie thinks I'm complicating my life by not believing in God. For her, having faith is easy, so why deprive yourself of it, why take unnecessary chances?

But Marie didn't mention God. As she'd never heard of agoraphobia, she began by listening to me, occasionally requesting clarifications and bursting into laughter when she realized how ridiculous and untenable agoraphobia could be. Her eyes filled with tears when I explained that I was unable to drive alone along the road between Fox Creek and La Hêtrière that leads into the Memramcook valley. I should mention that Marie weighs more than 250 pounds and that her tears were prompted mainly by the idea of being deprived of the excellent pies served at LeBlanc's restaurant across from the Saint-Joseph baseball field in the valley. She found it less of a problem that I couldn't bring myself to drive to Shediac for fear of having an attack on the highway.

"Just take the old road. It's a whole lot prettier."

⊚

Under the sign of Sagittarius, the ninth astrological house is the house of that higher spirit that inspires religion, law, science, ideals, and government. It includes philosophy, higher education, psychology, and all forms of study of the mind, notably through dreams and visions. The ninth house is the house of long mental voyages and intellectual speculation, of foreign lands and foreigners, and of long trips and high commerce. It's the house of expansion, of reaching out to the masses, as well as the house of advertising and publishing. The ninth house opens up a larger vision of life: it questions the meaning of death and aspires to describe the indescribable. The house of continuity, it ensures the preservation of heritage through rituals and symbols. The house of life's lessons, it fosters objectivity and knowledge.

⊚

Marie felt the need to understand. "Alright, but when it happens, what is it you're thinking is going to happen to you?"

"Hard to say. I just know that I feel real bad. My heart gets to beating a mile a minute, my legs go all rubbery, and I can hardly breathe. The first time, I thought I was about to have a heart attack. It's as though I'm about to faint or go crazy, one or the other. In an airplane, I'm afraid I'll start yelling or talking crazy and no one will understand."

Delirium worries psychiatrists far less than it does the general population, which is quick to brand someone as crazy as soon as he or she manifests the slightest loss of reason. In some cases, delirium is a relatively harmless manifestation of an acute psychological sensitivity, while in others it's at the root of how we relate to the world. Hence the importance of distinguishing between circumstantial delirium and what we might call true delirium by paying closer attention to the psychological state of the delirious person. For example, delirium is considered perfectly normal when it appears as the expression of a mood or emotional state. Announcing that you could eat a horse instead of saying you're hungry is the expression of a feeling of well-being or exaltation and has nothing to do with a delirious illness. Poetic licence is of the same order: we stretch, we exaggerate the real in order to express it more clearly or to render it more picturesque. In the same way, anyone who is excited or confused may rave or ramble. But such a person is almost sure to return to her senses once her emotional equilibrium is reestablished. Thus, considering her particular fragility, it would not be abnormal for an agoraphobe aboard an airplane to become delirious in mid-flight. Or to burst into tears. Such irrational behaviour does not extend into all facets of that individual's life, however, with the same permanence and profound insistence that it does in the lives of people suffering from delusions, fantasies, hallucinations, or paranoid psychoses. In short, when it comes to delirium, we are all granted some leeway. Each of us has a right to our small deliriums.

I had a feeling the airplane story would lead to some confusion.

"Sure, but isn't fear in airplanes claustrophobia?"

"It's all related. That's why psychologists nowadays talk about panic disorder with or without agoraphobia. In my case it's with. Trouble is, I can have an attack pretty much anytime, whenever I have some distance to travel. And it doesn't have to be far. It can happen on an empty street, in a swimming pool, at the beach, at a red light, or in a forest. And in any kind of vehicle, too. Almost anywhere. In the literature, they call it psychological distance." Marie was contemplating all this. I wanted to reassure her somehow. "Anyway, there's lots of folks worse off than me. There's some that never leave their house alone. Others can't even be alone at home. At Agoraphobes Anonymous, I even heard of a woman who walks on all fours in her house, just so she doesn't have to see outside when she passes a window."

"Lord in Heaven!"

"It's mostly women who've got it."

"How's that you call it again? Angoraphobia?"

"A. Agoraphobia. In the worst cases, it can lead to depression, alcoholism, or suicide."

"Well, sure, I guess it would."

◉

Phobias, or fears that develop into a system within the human psyche, belong to the family of anxiety neuroses. These arise and evolve in the affective aspect of the personality, just as psychosomatic disorders and psychoses do. Anxiety appears when there is a conflict between desire and fear — in Freud's words, it is born of the failed act — and acquires the status of a phobia when it becomes fixated on an idea, a situation, or an object that is mainly symbolic and reflects unacknowledged desires. Hence the power of attraction and fascination that the core of the phobia holds over its victim. Hence also the potential for the phobia to become the centre of the individual's thoughts, and even an obsession. In the end, it is avoidance behaviour that confirms a phobia. The affected individual will always flee from any situation that evokes the tumul-tuous conflict rooted in their unconscious, a conflict the management of which, even when it is inadequate, espe-cially when it is inadequate, requires an uncommon effort.

More than a hundred phobias have been catalogued, some having greater consequence than others. Some are relatively widespread, others may surprise at first but their potential is quickly recognized once you think about it: triskaidekaphobia, for example, the fear of seating thirteen people around a table; or autodysosmophobia, the fear of smelling bad; or even basophobia, the fear of having to walk. We can recognize the humour inherent in phobias without necessarily denigrating those who are terrorized by them.

IX

Marie wanted to help. "Sure, but isn't there some pill you could take?"

I didn't fault her for asking, but there was no easy answer. Of course, there are pills of every colour and kind. I didn't mention the little green pill they gave soldiers who were charged with dangerous missions during D-Day, a pill that caused instant death and was to be swallowed to avoid divulging secret information if they were captured by the enemy. Because, unlike me, Marie is easily upset, among other things by the idea of suicide. She might have concluded I was depressed when, in fact, I'm more angry than depressed.

I tried to explain to Marie that, since it's primarily women who suffer from agoraphobia, prescribing a tranquilizer seems like too easy a solution, like a Band-Aid on a wound, like a way to keep them quiet and to put off examining the root of the disease. Medication, in calming the effects of the illness, risks attenuating the search for a cause. I added that many agoraphobes detest medicines: exasperated at being so dependent on friends and family for their slightest movements, they can't bear the idea of further dependence. For them, no drug could ever be synonymous with a cure.

To make certain Marie understood, I told her about the spring, some fifteen minutes by car from our neighbourhood, where lots of people go to draw pure, clear water at no charge. Marie hadn't heard of the place.

"Well, as far as I'm concerned, that spring might as well be a bloody mountain. And yet, there are houses all along the road. Alright, it's not spectacular, but it's no brush land either. And though it's more of an Anglo place, it seems to me I ought to be able to go there anyhow." Marie sat perfectly still. I'd hit on the right topic. "Worst thing is, I can't stop thinking about it. I'd like to be able to go whenever I want, but I don't feel I can and it turns me inside out. I think about it every day. I try to get ready to go, I start weighing all the pros and cons, and in the end I just stay home because there are too many things against me. Either too many clouds, or not enough time, or too many Anglos out there, or the car could break down and I'd have no one to call, or there's nothing good on the radio, or nothing good in my life. There's always something or other to stop me going. It's pure madness, I tell you!"

Marie seemed to understand. "You ask me, I'd say you're thinking too hard on it."

"Probably."

". . ."

"Do you suppose a man would give himself so much trouble for a jug of water?"

The question took shape on Marie's forehead as she rested her hands, dripping with chicken fat, on the edge of her pans.

"If there was a commercial dispenser of spring water not far from home where you could fill up your jug in a flash for a couple of dollars, do you suppose a man would bother himself to go for water some place he knows he'll be scared?"

Marie didn't know what to say.

"And if a man couldn't even think about giving himself all that trouble, how could he even imagine the possibility of being scared?"

Marie eyed me quizzically. She wasn't sure she'd understood, but she had an idea. "You mean a man who can't see farther than his nose ain't smart enough to be afraid?" That was another way to put it. And Marie concluded, "No, I don't guess I know too many men'd give themselves such a heap of trouble just for a jug of water."

☙

Not all human beings are constituted in the same way; that is, they don't all have the same capacity to adapt. Genetic and sociocultural factors come into play as do the limits of perception. Difficulties in adapting can also arise from conditioning: women, for example, are more inclined to phobic neuroses than men are, perhaps because their place in society tends to be predetermined. Statistics show that anxiety generally takes the form of phobic neuroses in women, whereas men tend more toward alcoholism and drug addiction. As for agoraphobia, the fear of wide open spaces, women make up three quarters of those who suffer from it.

Phobias also tend to take root in adolescents and young adults. These sensitivities among young people are particularly revealing, especially about the transition from adolescence to adulthood. When adapting to adult life is too difficult, as is often the case in rapidly evolving societies, young people may simply refuse to grow up. But not all such refusals are signs of an inability to adapt. A refusal to adapt to a reality that one considers unhealthy can be a conscious decision and indicative of a social, rather than biological, malaise. As a given society evolves, it gives rise to new types of anxiety: the fear of flying, for example, appeared with the first commercial flights.

◎

Marie was beginning to know me. This wasn't the first time she'd read my mind. "You're going anyway, I hope."

". . ."

She looked me straight in the eye. "You've got to go. You wouldn't do that to us."

". . ."

"Don't even think about it. You're going, I tell you. There's got to be a way." And with that, she took the sieve full of chicken bones, shook it to drain the few last drops, and poured its contents mechanically into the organic recycling bin. "These new bins sure are convenient. Can't imagine how we made do without them."

◎

Bruegel must have been about twenty-three years old in 1551, when he embarked upon the traditional voyage to Italy that so many artists and thinkers of his era undertook in pursuit of Italianism, or the grace of ancient and distant beauty, which was in style at the time. Although he had recently been inducted into the guild of Saint Luke in Antwerp, Bruegel, like many of his fellow artists, must have had trouble earning a living during such a difficult economic period and, therefore, would have been easily persuaded to make the classic voyage in order to complete his training. During this period, historians tell us, Antwerp was crawling with artists: they were certainly far more numerous than bakers or butchers, whose livelihoods were quite secure because their products were essential.

It is also possible that Bruegel undertook the trip at the suggestion of his publisher, Jerome Cock, who owned an engraving studio and one of the most active print shops in the Netherlands. Cock hoped to produce a series of prints of great alpine landscapes and may have convinced Bruegel to make the trip in order to sketch the countryside along the way, which it seems Bruegel did. A number of these drafts were discovered in the works of other artists employed by Cock, who published his *Great Landscapes* series in 1555.

But all of these very good reasons to go would not have sufficed had Bruegel himself not been curious about new landscapes and people. Whatever the case, his decision to undertake the pilgrimage and the manner in which the experience subsequently permeated his work has led some to conclude that the voyage marks the true beginning of his artistic career. Like so many details of Bruegel's life, the dates of his departure from Antwerp and his return to his native land are uncertain, but it would appear that the trip lasted three years. Whether he went alone or accompanied and the precise itinerary that led him to Sicily remain mysteries. Our knowledge of the historical period suggests that he covered an average of fifty kilometres a day on horseback, that he rode mostly during the day through the silence of the countryside, and that he was often obliged to stop to let military troops pass.

@

One of the most important psychological assets humans can possess is the ability to feel completely at ease in their environment. Any fear of this environment leads inexorably to a decline and confinement, even a sort of slavery. These unfortunate consequences are probably the reason fear has taken on a negative connotation, since as an emotion, fear is really neutral, simply a reaction to a given situation.

The affective dimension of personality, from which fear emanates, is one of the three great components of the human psyche: the first includes cognitive activities, or processes relating to consciousness and knowledge; the second encompasses affective processes, those that relate to feelings and emotions; the third is comprised of the conative processes that deal with the dynamics of human motivation. These three components represent the forces at work in the processes of knowledge, feeling, and action.

Emotion is not easily analyzed but, as its etymological root indicates, the term implies a movement, a displacement. In the best of cases, emotional movement triggers a kind of internal reorganization of the senses, which enables one to adapt more or less rapidly to the environment. More than simply a matter of behaviour, emotions are really a human being's adaptive response to the environment. In cases of behavioural disorders, emotions are nothing more than an inappropriate response to a stimulus. Excessively difficult tasks, novelty, surprise, and overmotivation are, generally, the causes of emotional behaviour. Often an emotion corresponds to the difference between the requirements of a situation and the means at our disposal to respond. Even too great a desire to respond appropriately to a situation can negatively affect an individual's behaviour or efficiency.

There are those who believe that Bruegel began his voyage by dallying, leaving what was then the Netherlands near the end of 1551 and then slowly crossing France from north to south. There is proof of his passing through Lyons and one of his paintings may be a view of Vienne, which is not far from Lyons. He appears to have descended the Rhône valley, with a possible detour to Briançon and to the little village of Pont-de-Cervières, around August 15, 1552, more than six months after his departure. He would then have gone through Avignon to reach Marseilles, where he embarked upon a ship that sailed along the coast of Italy to the Strait of Messina. It was along this route that Bruegel presumably drew a live sketch of Reggio in flames, a Calabrian town torched by the Turks in 1552. He would have landed in Sicily and visited Palermo before making his way up the Italian boot as far as Naples. He probably passed through Fondi en route to Rome, where he stayed for some time in 1553 and from where he made several excursions, notably to Tivoli. He is then said to have stopped in Florence, visited Pisa and the Emilia region, and befriended the great geographer Scipio Fabius in Bologna. It is possible that during this time, Bruegel was travelling with another Antwerp painter, Martin de Vos, who lived in Italy from 1552 to 1558.

Probably Bruegel waited until the spring of 1554 to cross the Alps, a perilous journey to undertake in winter. He took advantage of the good weather to explore the mountain chain from one end to the other. All signs point to his having visited the Dolomites and the Tyrol as far as Innsbruck, travelled through the Grisonides and Saint Gothard Pass, and reached Geneva and the shores of Lake Leman. Though no one knows the exact date of Bruegel's return to Antwerp, all agree that he was there in 1555.

X

TERRY THIBODEAU PRESUMED everyone felt the way he did, a bit lonely, never quite like everyone else. Since he'd always felt this way, it never occurred to him to fuss over it. He carried the feeling naturally, just as he carried his Saint Christopher medal around his neck.

Terry Thibodeau remembered the day his third-grade teacher gave him the medal. The young woman knew that Terry liked the story of this saint best of all. Terry was impressed with Saint Christopher's idea of helping people, especially children, to cross rivers. For a long time, he'd imagined the saint standing by an abandoned bridge on the Wisener River, ready to take him, Terry, on his shoulders, if ever he went by there again. He could even picture, some way along the shore, the small cabin in which Saint Christopher slept and kept his basic provisions. Terry didn't know if the Wisener froze in winter and he hardly dared think what happened to Saint Christopher if it did: did he hole up in his cabin until spring or did he pack up and continue his saintly duties somewhere farther south? Since Terry could only imagine the Crossing Saint barefoot and wearing a light tunic, it seemed cruel to think of him at his post in winter, sitting in the snow waiting for a passenger or wading through icy water between two snowbound shores.

⊚

Under the sign of Cancer, the fourth astrological house is, strictly speaking, the house of houses; that is, it relates to property, to the comfort and improvement of the home. The house of private life and reclusion, it also encompasses hidden treasures and mined riches. As the house where life begins, it includes heredity and ancestry, psychological roots and atavisms, or those needs and drives that emanate from the depths of the unconscious, and that also often give rise to works of art, music, and poetry. The fourth house expresses the weight of our destiny at birth, with all the assistance and obstacles it carries. It's the house of all that we inherit at birth and of our familial environment during childhood. It's the house of good and bad feelings, of attachments, of the subjective self as the foundation for one's personality and interior life. The fourth house ensures the passage from childhood to adult life. In that sense, it is the generator of power. House of life's beginnings, the fourth house is also that of life's end, of posthumous celebrity, and of one's burial place.

⊚

Even had he tried, Terry Thibodeau would have found it difficult to pinpoint the reasons for his feeling of solitude. He'd had plenty of support from friends and family during his childhood in Dieppe on Lafrance Street, between Gauvin Road and Champlain Street, not far from the Second Stream, beside the Champlain Body Shop his father and

brothers operated. During his adolescence, not being especially interested in dented sheet metal, he'd found a job as
a bagger at the Champlain Place supermarket. He could
probably have made a career of it but the motivation was
lacking. After high school and failed attempts at community
college and university, Terry ran out of ideas: most trades
didn't interest him and those that did seemed out of
reach. Actually, he couldn't even have named one. What
he wanted was something inexpressible, incomprehensible.
He struggled along for several years, looking for a job at a
time when jobs were increasingly scarce, and then one day
he got lucky.

An escape from frustration for some, a longing for new
experiences for others, tourism today allows the individual
human being to enter into a new relationship with the
world. This victory over space, which is the result of a
victory over time, allows each of us to create a kind of personal geography of the world, a geography defined by
explorations that reconcile the myth of the traveller with our
unconscious image of what constitutes a voyage. This
attempt to correspond to ancient and modern archetypes, to
link up different times by travelling through space, is not so
different from the human dream of immortality.

As it rattles and breaks open societies by redefining
social relations, tourism changes how we think and make
sense of things in as yet uncharted ways. For, everywhere
tourists go, they remain outside of the political and of
politics. This temporary suspension of responsibility is
undoubtedly good for vacationers, who are generally trying
to escape the demands of a highly industrialized society,
but it has entirely different repercussions on those societies
that depend on tourism for their survival. As a result,

the new existential norms attributable to tourism have opened new areas for study in economics, the science of logical action, and in sociology, the science of alogical action.

In psychology, when travel is not simply discredited as pure escapism, it is seen as a reflection of the interior quest, the search for a centre, a ground of truth and peace. To the vast movement of people in our planetary space, psychology posits a corresponding and equally modern interior voyage of the individual into him or herself, a descent into the unconscious. In a curious reversal, the psychology of tourism and travel leads to a rereading of several classical myths: in particular, those of Poseidon, or the rush to water; Minerva, or continuing popular education; Sisyphus, or the impossibility of leisure; and Heliopolis, or the city of reassuring portents. Another mythical image, that of desertification or ecological imbalance, also comes into play and is linked with the idea of collective disaster. All this means that alongside those who travel unselfconsciously, there are also those, mostly women, who struggle to understand their behaviour and wonder why they feel like tourists — individuals at once complex and suffering from complexes — five kilometres from home.

❦

Baron of oil and paper and pretty well all their subsidiary industries, from shipping and trucking, to newsprint, to toilet paper, not to mention frozen vegetables (which are also rich in fibre and sold to the proletariat by the thousands), the Irving multinational corporation had recently restored the dune of Bouctouche. And like God when He created the world, the Irvings saw that it was indeed good. They now searched for another opportunity to do good. They forged ahead therefore, as they had when they built the upscale ecotourism centre, with its convenient cottages for tourists who came unprepared or lacked relatives, along the dune on the beach. The cottages were clustered in small groups — tourists tend to be gregarious — near the water or along the bicycle path that encircles the greater Bouctouche region from the back of the bay into the Pays de la Sagouine, a region made famous by Antonine Maillet's Acadian characters. All along the route a number of scenes inspired by the work of Maillet were enacted. As these performances were well received, the Irving family made plans to build a theatre school in Bouctouche, dedicated to the roles engendered by Madame Maillet's work, and meant to preserve Bouctouche and all its people, both fictional and real, for posterity.

The ecotourism centre was rolling along splendidly, just like a bicycle wheel all shining and well-greased. The smooth and efficient planning of activities succeeded in extending the summer season beyond its natural inclination and allowed some one hundred people to accumulate enough stamps to get back on UI, unemployment insurance, a program that some clever national strategists had unnamed in order to erase all notions of leisure or free time and renamed EI, employment insurance, to promote a spirit of enterprise and productive labour. Thanks to the Irving empire's intuition about its tenth house, almost no one had time to brandish picket signs in protest against the insensitivity and inaction of governments in the matter of job creation. And in the excitement over the promised opening of the Bouctouche École Nationale, anger even died down over the closure of the theatre department at the Université de Moncton.

Sisyphus or the myth of impossible leisure time. In a dream one January night, I take a pleasure trip to New York with a friend. But once there, I am called to work: it seems I am to replace a truck driver who has fallen ill. I'm to drive his trailer truck to some other American state, a trip which will take about a week. Somehow, the assignment doesn't strike me as abnormal; it's as though I were already a trucker or as though I knew how to and could do anything. Then I see the mammoth truck in question, parked between skyscrapers on a narrow street, boxed in among a dozen other vehicles in dense traffic. I also see all the poles and street signs I'm likely to hit as I try to drive off this street. I realize the enormity and absurdity of the task. I realize that what is being asked of me makes no sense, that I don't have the required skills. So I go back to my employer and explain my concerns. Three guys in a small basement office listen and quickly concur. They decide to find someone else to take care of the truck. All this is done calmly and reasonably. I leave the tiny office, find my friend in the street, and continue our trip without further ado. What strikes me about this dream is the ease with which normal and absurd situations coincide. Its harmonious denouement makes it a good dream, and yet I can't help wondering why it's necessary to go through it all.

XI

THE ENORMOUS POPULAR success of the Bouctouche dune project encouraged the Irvings to continue to restructure and recreate the world around them. Their gaze turned quite naturally toward Moncton, where the mere acquisition of a hockey team no longer satisfied them. They soon found a challenge worthy of their ambitions: returning the infamous Petitcodiac River to its former glory. A team of top-grade engineers was assembled and supported by biologists, historians, recreationists, and businesspeople. All of these people worked for more than two years to plan the project. Toward the end of the meticulous and ambitious gestation period, heavy machinery began to appear here and there along the banks of the river, waiting to be put to use.

The plan was essentially to enlarge the Petitcodiac riverbed and install ultrasensitive drift controls in order to protect the route tourist boats would take between Beaumont and downtown Moncton. Although the tidal bore had diminished over the years, the currents remained so strong that no boat risked sailing the Petitcodiac anymore for fear of getting stuck in the increasingly invasive mudbanks. The danger was greatest in the area of the river's bend at the juncture of Dieppe and Moncton, where the river makes a ninety-degree turn. The engineers perfected an electronic current-detection system to guarantee safe passage through the drifting currents at all times. The Irvings were clearly prepared to spend what it took to complete this highly sophisticated technological project, which even attracted the attention of the designers of Montréal's Olympic Stadium roof.

As for the excursions themselves, they would be rewarding in every way. In the boats, natural and technological forces would confront one another on a wall of screens projecting images of both the real and the virtual. The ecology and history of the river would also get their share of attention: the biologists were hard at work preparing presentations while the historical interpreters were busy rehearsing re-enactments of Native life and Acadian settlement, from the arrival of the settlers at the end of the seventeenth century to the final attempts at deporting them in 1758. The route would be dotted with observation posts and landing spots. A gigantic aboiteau, or sluice gate, large enough for the tourist boats to pass through, would be constructed to educate visitors and Acadians alike about the ingenuity of the ancient dike system constructed to protect the land from devastating river floods. There was even talk that the boat cruises could eventually be extended as far as the Bay of Fundy. In which case, the cruise would last several days and have its first night stopover near the famous Hopewell Rocks, where the Petitcodiac and Memramcook rivers empty into the Shepody estuary. The following day, the visitors would circumnavigate Capes Maringouin and Enragé and camp in Fundy National Park. The proposed voyage would require more imposing vessels than those that sailed exclusively on the Petitcodiac but, in keeping with the corporate philosophy that had brought them success, the Irvings relished the possibility of calling on the services of their Saint John shipyard and ensuring that the wheels of their numerous companies continued to turn.

◎

Under the sign of Capricorn, the tenth astrological house is the house of careers or professions, of places of business and employers, of the relationship to authority and the authority one exercises in one's profession. In spite of disruptions, one's professional life may evolve favourably, but it is always subject to reversals and paradoxes. House of major projects and social tests, the tenth house includes all things relating to public life: reputation, popularity, ambition, savoir-faire, credit, prestige, honours, titles, and rank. Professional activities, whether imposed or voluntary, also play a role in establishing one's name and public image. This is the house of what will be remembered of a life's work, of glory and fame, of a career as it contributes to the public image; it's the house of services rendered and of one's love for the world. This house determines one's ability to enjoy life fully. The house of accumulated accomplishments and of the final accomplishment, it also includes, to a degree, the fear of not being able to fulfill our expectations of ourselves. The tenth house represents the work we do to increase our own and other people's self-awareness. From this house, we also get an indication of a child's expectations of her parents.

◎

It was her aunt and godmother, Émerentienne Goguen, who on her return from one of her numerous trips (this one to

France) gave little Carmen Després a magnificently illus-
trated book entitled *The Great Deltas*. This particular aunt
was always trying to make up for her hedonistic side by
engaging and attempting to engage others in things educa-
tional. Thus it was that in the months following her group
excursion to France, the extravagant Émerentienne Goguen
could speak of nothing else but the Bouches-du-Rhône
region, which she managed somehow to dip like dry bis-
cuits into every conversation.

Carmen Després did not hold her fun-loving aunt's pecu-
liarities against her. She never imagined her aunt could be
otherwise. So she leafed through the book without the
slightest reservation, discovering breathtaking aerial views
of parcelled lands that seemed to be coming apart but that
were actually building their foundations, consolidating from
below, in order to emerge one day from the water and take
another bite out of the ocean. In an effort to better understand deltas, she stared for hours at the rivulets of water that
descended from the mountains to become sometimes docile
and sometimes torrential rivers which, more often than not,
adopted the longest and least likely routes to reach the sea.
At times, she wished she could get right inside the picture to
smell the air and spirit of these prodigious waterways.

The Irving family's directive was crystal clear: every effort
was to be made to provide young people with job opportunities at the planned Petitcodiac River Historical and
Ecological Park. Terry Thibodeau was one of the lucky ones
since his unemployment dossier perfectly matched the type
they were looking for: he had been without work for a min-
imum of two years and had been on welfare for a long time.
They put him through a battery of tests to determine if he

had what it took, first, to complete the boat operator's training course and, then, to pass the final test. The title of operator had been chosen over navigator because the latter was judged too strong considering that all the boats were equipped with a steering-assistance system. No one wanted to anger the real captains, the local legends who continued to court true danger and who had a tendency to rise up in anger over the slightest thing.

On his twenty-fourth birthday, December 12, the twelfth day of the twelfth month, Terry received the telephone call that would at last give his life direction. He was to present himself at the manpower office on Main Street in Moncton, across from Jones Lake, where he would be given all the details of a very interesting job. He went without much hope, underwent all the formalities, again without much hope, was accepted into the training program and completed it, still without much hope; after all, he had had some life experience. But this time was the right time; everything went as smoothly as a knife through butter. And so it was that barely eight months later, on a fine August day, Terry Thibodeau found himself seated in front of the controls of a tourist boat in the middle of the brown river, and was obliged to acknowledge his personal transformation: he had a job that satisfied him, for the time being; he'd learned to talk to people, an activity he no longer scorned even though they were only tourists; and he had begun to read again.

Product of the three planes of space and the four cardinal points, the number twelve symbolizes both the internal complexity of the world and the celestial vault, which is divided into twelve sections, the twelve signs of the zodiac. We find its symbolic power in all the great civilizations, as well as among lesser-known peoples like the Dogons and Bambaras of Mali for whom the three and four correspond to the male and female elements, which together add up to the static number seven and multiply to produce the dynamic number twelve, and thus represent the perpetual becoming of the individual being and the universe. Twelve is the action number, and it represents accomplishments and the completed cycle. We find it often in the Jewish and Christian holy texts, where it symbolizes perfection. Multiplied by itself, the number twelve is said to lead to nothing less than plenitude and paradise.

Terry Thibodeau was preparing his boat, the *Beausoleil-Broussard*, for the day's first excursion when a dark young woman appeared at the end of the pier.

"Yoohoo!"

Terry looked up. She looked familiar but he couldn't be sure.

She spoke again. "Not too many people today."

"August 15 was yesterday." Terry checked his watch. It was barely nine o'clock and already the site had been cleaned and cleared of the main installations from the previous day's celebrations of Acadia's national day. Though a dozen or so Acadian flags continued to flap in the wind.

"I mean for river cruises."

"People aren't used yet to coming when the tide is up."

"Oh." The young woman studied the site, the green spaces and flowerbeds, the little concession stands and information panels. "Is it really Irving did all this, then?"

"The park, you mean? Pretty much, yeah."

"What's the idea?"

Terry didn't think the girl really expected a reply. "Did you want to take the tour?"

"Don't know. It is kind of a nice day."

"The next cruise leaves in half an hour. You'll have to sign up over there in the little booth."

The young woman turned to look at the deserted booth. "Is there no one else?"

"All depends. There's some that buy their tickets early and then take a stroll in the streets of Le Coude, have a coffee or something, while they're waiting."

"Oh." The young woman looked at the river. She didn't seem in any hurry to make up her mind.

Terry waited a bit before telling her, as politely as possible, "They don't really like you hanging around on this part of the pier."

"Oh?"

XII

I KNEW I HAD TO decolonize myself, to free myself, but I had no idea where to start. I felt enormous and divided, like Africa: weakened, invaded, badly coordinated, primitive, and paradoxical. I didn't even know what to be anymore, what exactly to want. It had become almost impossible to take a step in any direction. Even the streets of my neighbourhood had become alien and menacing, somehow unreal. I got in the habit of going everywhere by car, even to the corner store. Even so, I avoided certain streets during rush hour for fear of being immobilized in traffic and I never dared to leave town alone. I knew my limits. In spite of this though, I managed to live and appear normal. That was perhaps what was most troubling.

Three other people approached the *Beausoleil-Broussard* a few minutes before its departure. Terry was relieved. He hadn't been looking forward to doing the entire tour alone with this young woman who had already asked him his name, his age, and his opinion on the book he was reading.

"So what's your name, then?"

His name was sewn on the front of his shirt, but she was too far away to read it. He felt embarrassed somehow about telling her his name. "Terry."

"Terry what?"

"Thibodeau."

"Oh."

Silence. The pause was critical. It put Terry at ease and made him feel like continuing the conversation. "How about you, then? What's your name?"

"Carmen."

"Carmen what?"

"Després."

"And where're you from?"

"Grande-Digue."

"I thought they was all Bourgeois in Grande-Digue."

"They're a good number. The Després come from Cocagne, really. My father moved to Grande-Digue to get away from his family."

The ironic reply made Terry laugh. Cocagne was only a few kilometres from Grande-Digue.

There was another pause before she continued, "What's that you're reading, then?"

"Oh, it's just a book." Normally Terry would have left it at that but today his reply seemed too brief and not particularly bright. He tried to lengthen it a bit. "It's about the number twelve, all the ways that number exists."

"And do you like it?"

"It's okay."

Another brief silence. Carmen eyed the expanse of water before her. "How old are you, then?"

"Why?"

"Just to know. I'd say you're twenty-six."

"Twenty-four."

"Twice twelve."

"Exactly." Terry had answered nonchalantly but this girl made him laugh inside. "And how old are you, then?"

"Thirty. I look younger though, don't I?"

"Well, yeah . . . sort of."

"Is thirty any good?"

"Thirty?"

"Yeah, thirty. Twice twelve plus six."

"Oh! Well, I don't know. Maybe. How do you like it?"

"Oh! I like it just fine."

@

For example, I would never have boarded one of those tourist boats that sail along the Petitcodiac. Not in a million years! I'd only have to set foot on board for their renowned remote controls to break down. But even there, I could pass for normal. So many people boycott or would like to boycott the Irvings that my own resistance would go unnoticed. The fact that they're retrieving a part of our history means nothing. The Irvings could give us back all of New France, we still wouldn't trust them. That's the way it is.

It's no different in Shediac. With all the people on the beach in summer time, I can stay on the sand or go in the water; either way, I look perfectly normal. No one has to know I swim only at high tide because at low tide you have to walk miles (I'm exaggerating) in a foot of water and if I had an episode and fainted, I'd drown. That's a new fear from last summer. New ones crop up like that now and then. When I overcome one fear, another appears. Often I can feel them coming in my stomach. The worst places are those huge multi-floor bookstores they have in big cities. All those books do something to my intestines. When I see them, I wonder why I write.

On the return trip, Terry hoped the young woman with all the questions would be quiet for a bit. He liked her offhand manner but earlier she'd stretched him to the limit. He wasn't sure he'd managed all right.

"Do you suppose there might be a way to prove the Petitcodiac is the opposite of a delta?"

Terry wasn't sure he understood what Carmen Després was asking.

She reformulated her question. "I mean, a river that fills up, mightn't it be the opposite of a delta, which is a river that empties into the sea and fills up the sea while it empties itself?" Terry didn't know what to answer, but Carmen Després was determined. "What I mean is that instead of the river filling up the sea, it's the sea that fills the river. That's all, and wouldn't that be the reverse of a delta, then?"

Terry was a bit shaken. She seemed to know what she was talking about. He thought back to all the readings he'd done during his training. "Well, you may be right, only I would've thought the opposite of a delta was an estuary. Like Shepody Bay, for example."

Carmen Després didn't know how to explain herself, but that didn't stop her from trying again. "Well, alright then, but couldn't it be that a river that fills up with silt . . . if the same thing happened on the edge of the coast, it would be like a delta? Seems to me, a person could prove that."

"Well, maybe so, I'm sure I don't know. And what would be the point of proving something like that?"

"Don't know. None maybe. Sometimes, you just need to prove something."

Then one day, I decide it's gone on long enough and I make up my mind. I grab my plastic water bottles and get in the car. I'm already up to my neck in this mess, which no one suspects but which has nevertheless become my lot. I cling to every ounce of self-confidence, I gather up all my courage, I start the car; in short, I do all that must be done and I'm off. Before I'm even past the city limits, I've already undone my seatbelt to breathe more easily, to breathe from my diaphragm as all anxiety manuals instruct you to do. A lovely song is playing on the radio. This helps. On the other hand, sometimes it's silence I need. Nothing is predictable. Sometimes neither works. Sometimes every little thing is too much and nothing suffices: an innocent thought, a slight emotion, and I'm gone. So I slow down, I take my foot off the gas. At times, when I have the presence of mind to advance slowly, things fall back into place, take on more reasonable proportions, and it becomes possible to continue going forward. The error may be to want to go too fast, or simply to want too much. This is what I tell myself in the shopping centre, when I lose my courage in those unending corridors, when this thing wells up in me and pushes me once again toward despair. I tell myself everything is all right, everything is fine, I just want to buy myself a pair of socks, I have every right, and there's no hurry.

At the end of the cruise, instead of disembarking, Carmen Després stationed herself at the bow of the boat and studied the mouth of Hall's Creek. Terry kept his distance. He was afraid of being drawn into her delta thing again. Not wanting to appear rude by asking her to get off, he pretended to be busy adjusting the *Beausoleil-Broussard*'s cathode screens.

After a while, the young woman from Grande-Digue marched to the plank, then changed her mind and turned back toward Terry. "Back there, when you talked about the fish in the river, did you say there were still some?"

"Truth is, there's only the eel, really. There's other kinds but you don't want to go and eat them. Once, there was plenty of smelt and shad, even salmon and trout. All that's gone now, on account of the causeway down there."

Carmen had been watching Terry while he spoke. She'd measured his profile against the brown of the water, the green of the shore, and the blue of the sky. As a result, she was taken by surprise when silence came so quickly on the heels of his words. Looking at the causeway, she tried to think of something to add, to show Terry that his words hadn't fallen on deaf ears. "Well, I guess so. Those gates aren't exactly wide."

3

Gallimard . . . Hot Stuff

XIII

ÉLIZABETH IS LYING in the arms of Hans in an unmade bed. Dawn fills the white-walled room. In the distance the sea rumbles, or perhaps it's just the wind. Élizabeth isn't quite ready to open her eyes. Hans, on the other hand, is wide-awake.

"So, you don't like labyrinths?"

"Not particularly, no."

"They're complex universes."

"Is that why one ought to like them?"

"It's not required. Some people like them naturally."

Hans had hesitated a while before initiating this morning conversation. Now that it was started he saw no reason to hold back. "Do you like chickens?"

"I like that they peck and lay eggs."

Hans uses the formal *vous* when he addresses Élizabeth. In a way, he dreads the moment when they will lapse into the familiar *tu*. For now, he enjoys this formality of love between them. "Do you like volcanoes?"

"Not especially. But, yes, a bit."

"And deltas?"

"Yes."

"Even though there's something labyrinthine about them?"

"Yes. I like them on account of the water."

"Do you like diamonds?"

"No, not really. They're too shiny."

⊚

One night at the end of August, Terry Thibodeau walked alone into one of the town's billiard parlours. Establishments of the sort had sprouted like mushrooms lately, turning the once suspect game into a perfectly respectable pastime for everybody, including women. There were even more and more children in the pool halls. Some were learning to play; others, who were still in swaddling clothes or recently out of diapers, simply tagged along with their parents.

This broad democratization of the game annoyed Terry, who chose a table out of the way, out of sight of the crowd, not because he was a poor player — on the contrary, he'd been a champion — but because he didn't like the attention his skill attracted. He barely had time to break before a waitress was at his table.

"And would you be wanting a drink, then?"

Terry instantly recognized the voice. "Oh . . . well hello! No, I've only come to play a few games."

" . . . "

Carmen Després didn't seem in any hurry to move on.

Terry felt the need to say something. "I didn't know you worked here. I come in sometimes when I've got nothing to do."

"I've only just started. I worked in Shediac before."

All of a sudden the walls began to shake to some particularly tribal music. The bass and drums drowned out everything else. Carmen rolled her eyes. "The worst is the music. I'll go change it. Is there something you'd like to hear, then?"

Terry thought for two seconds. "Have you got any Tom Waits?"

Carmen nodded her approval and left.

Under the sign of Leo, the fifth astrological house is the house of vital energy extended into the next generation through either children or artistic, literary, or scientific works. It includes political life and social affairs as well as the fine arts. The fifth house is the house of individual originality and the need for creative self-expression. The house of children and procreation, it also extends to education and the emotional life, and to all affairs of the heart, including love affairs. A sense of play, the ability to choose frivolity, to let yourself be distracted and forget the serious side of life, is also highly present in this house: sometimes it is manifested in small pleasures, hobbies, sports, or vacations and sometimes simply through attending the theatre or a concert or a social gathering. Gambling and games of chance can also be found in this house, along with financial speculation, donations, and gifts. House of risk, the fifth house also fosters experimentation in the realms of power. It pushes one to dare, to develop one's creative powers beyond simple ardour and the primal drives and in spite of initial awkwardness, shyness, or lack of savoir-faire. Through the pleasure of creation, the fifth house calls on us to risk our ego and learn to shine.

Carmen Després had been closely linked to the pool craze. Her father, a businessman, had seen it coming and begun to manufacture billiards equipment in Grande-Digue. Over fifteen years, the Diamond Billiards brand had gradually made its mark throughout North America, and its mastermind had been crowned businessman of the year at least six times in the process.

Carmen Després played a part in her father's success and prosperity. She had sat as youth representative on the committee responsible for renovating the Grande-Digue parish centre. The committee had valiantly defended the purchase of two pool tables, despite conservative parishioners who opposed the idea and feared the game would foster corruption and idleness. After the centre opened, Carmen prevailed several times upon her father to join her in a game of billiards, even though he had never so much as laid a hand on a pool cue before in his life.

Carmen, who had by then already received and read *The Great Deltas*, noticed, each time she broke, that the balls separated in a traditional deltaic pattern, the result perhaps of not quite having the knack others had of firing the balls off in all directions. After her first stroke of the cue, the balls came apart without much vigour, rolling here and there lazily, some of them remaining entirely unmoved by the break. And each time, Carmen wondered aloud at the jagged triangular shape her shot had produced, and each time, her father paused to contemplate with her the deltaic shape laid out over the cloth, moved as he was by his daughter's naïve joy in the midst of a room decorated with Metallica posters and little, knitted, woollen hearts of Jesus. There would have been posters of the rock group Slaughter, but they had been categorically rejected by a majority of parishioners.

The most brilliant of all precious stones, the diamond shines even in the dark, or almost. The slightest flicker of light is sufficient to set it ablaze. But it is probably the diamond's hardness that has made it the symbol of love: a diamond is unalterable; only its own dust can wear it down and then just to a degree. Diamond cutting, which renders the diamond even more brilliant, is accomplished by vigorously rubbing the gem with diamond dust, an operation that requires a great deal of time and precision. Diamond cutting attained a level of perfection with the brilliant "modern" cut of fifty-eight facets that was developed at the beginning of the twentieth century and was based on the "full" cut of the previous century. Other factors come into play in evaluating the excellence of a diamond: its limpidity (more poetically called its water), its colour, and, of course, its weight. The weight of a diamond is measured in carats. The diamond carat, unlike the gold carat, is a quantitative rather than a qualitative measurement.

Terry Thibodeau found Carmen Després more docile that evening than she'd been in his boat on the Petitcodiac. Although this was reassuring to a point, he kept an eye on her nonetheless, in part because there was something about her slightly rebellious attitude that appealed to him. He watched her from the corner of his eye as he sank balls. She seemed to be doing everything: waiting tables, handing out the racks of balls, tidying up behind the counter, barking out orders, disappearing, reappearing, so that it was hard to tell exactly what her role was in the place. Having lost sight of her, Terry focused on his game and momentarily forgot her.

"Nice shot!"

Terry tried not to blush but failed. "Where did you come from? I never saw you coming."

"Oh? So, you were looking out for me, were you?"

Terry felt his blood rise to his ears. He didn't usually blush for so little. "I wanted a beer all of a sudden."

"And what sort of beer?"

"Oh, I don't know. There're too many sorts these days. Why don't you just bring me what you like, makes no difference to me."

XIV

IT WASN'T THE overwhelming brilliance of the diamond that impressed Hans. Several times, he'd held the small stone between his fingers and let it drop on the cloth the merchant had spread over the counter. Each time, the stone flashed a thousand flames but, in the end, this game became dull. No, it was something else that interested him. Something that had nothing to do with the stone's aesthetic value. He dropped the stone again and this time Hans had the impression of throwing dice, which made him think of the chance workings of light and wealth. Now he felt he was getting somewhere. Holding onto this notion of the chance workings of light and wealth, he left the shop feeling happy.

Carmen Després returned with a Moosehead Green on her tray. Not being particularly partial to all the new brands of beer herself, she hadn't made much of an effort. But she liked the green bottle with a touch of red; it reminded her of Christmas.

Terry didn't have time to get money out of his pocket.

"Nope, it's on me. A gift."

Nor did Terry have time to protest, for Carmen was already serving the people who'd started playing at the table next to his.

⊚

The idea of the chance workings of light and wealth stayed with Hans. It was as though the concept had somehow opened the world to him, prompting something new, something entirely original. A feeling of lightness had come over him. Strangely, that tiny diamond he'd held between his fingers had simplified everything. Life had changed. The thing that was missing had appeared. Had he been searching for it a long time? Hans couldn't say. Had he hoped for it or had he given up hoping? He had no idea. He'd been occupied, preoccupied. His mind had been elsewhere. Today it had all come together. It had become something else within him. He had become. The becoming had taken place, had taken hold. As though by some miracle. As though it were possible.

⊚

Carmen and Terry began to see each other more often.

"Yesterday, on my boat, there was a fellow by the name of Absence Léger."

Carmen eyed Terry skeptically.

"I'm telling you. I didn't believe it either. So I listened real close, and I'm telling you, they were calling him Absence all day long."

"Must have been Absconce. Absconce Léger. There was a woman down our way by that name."

"No, I tell you. I'm sure this was Absence. Absence Léger."

"..."

"It sure is bugging me. I can't stop thinking about it."

@

Afternoon dream in the living room of an apartment whose windows are wide-open to a gentle summer rain: an enormous dark granite cube balances on the peak of a mountain. The edges of the cube are rounded but granular, like the rest of its surface. My gaze somehow penetrates the opacity of the stone. In the centre of the block is a huge uncut diamond. From the outside there is no hint of its presence. And yet there it is, an unseen treasure. What's striking is the contrast between the massive and perfectly structured cube and its interior, all angles of light and lightness. What's striking is the progressive transformation of the granite, the secret reconfiguration that has taken place.

When a diamond appears in a dream, its clarity, solidity, maturity, and perfection become somewhat petrified qualities. In the dream, the diamond seems to take on the properties we associate with crystals, living matter capable of growth. Its limpidity seems to have the ability to contain and engender everything. The dreamer then becomes aware of a repressed energy, as the diamond symbolizes the tension between a rush toward perfection and the promise of an explosion. This awareness is like a readjustment of poles, particularly those of fixedness and flexibility, of perfection and simplicity.

@

In the beginning, Terry and Carmen had a rather odd way of speaking to each other. During the day, listening to them, one might have concluded they were getting on each other's nerves.

"Hey . . . you're wearing red today!"

"You've got good eyesight."

"It's the first time I've seen you in red. Suits you."

Later, in the midst of a September silence, as he sat on a sunlit terrace, Terry added, "Acadians have always fancied red. Only, not having much of it to spare, they took to wearing it in little bits and pieces. Sometimes, they wove it into other materials just to make it last."

". . ."

"Well, that's what I read, anyhow."

With a slightly exasperated look, Carmen hauled on her cigarette and sighed, "I'm not looking forward to winter. Not one bit."

At night, the subjects they had touched on during the day resurfaced.

"Well, and what colours did they wear then, if there wasn't much red?"

"The only dyes they had were green and black."

"And how is it they had no red, then?"

"Don't know. When they did get some, it was from the English. The redcoats. Could be they tore those coats right off English backs."

". . ."

". . ."

". . ."

"Have you read the Bible?"

"No. Tried once. Pretty much unreadable."

"Well, do you suppose a person could live their whole life without reading the Bible? I mean, without knowing what it all means, the road to Damocles and the sword of Damascus?"

"Sure looks that way."

XV

AND THEN, AT SOME POINT, one gets fed up with personal growth. There's a limit to always trying to improve or surpass oneself. It's exhausting and eventually useless. So I told myself I might as well give up and accept my limitations instead of making myself sick over them. Accept the insurmountable. Accept not being able to go farther. And be content. Be proud of having come this far and leave it to others, our sons and daughters, to take up the baton and break new ground in their own ways. Accept the slow progress of human evolution. Accept my place in that slow progress. Let it be simply a condition of existence, and let that condition be good too, and not always negative, a diminishment of myself.

That day, I set out with my water jugs for the spring, but I halted resolutely in the middle of town at a hardware store that had recently installed a spring water dispenser. I was proud of myself, my decision, my cunning, my delinquency. I could justify it all, explain it all: it was right to encourage those resourceful folks who'd actually succeeded in bringing the spring closer to town and in enabling more people to benefit from it; here was a useful service that deserved to survive, and I'd be a fool not to make use of it myself; I had better things to do than to waste my time panicking over wild imaginings in the empty countryside, I ought instead to make it my duty to partake of the communal fountain in the company of my fellow citizens. It would bring me a lot closer to putting an end to my fear than would setting myself more or less insignificant challenges. And that's when, a full jug in one hand and an empty one in the other, I saw Camil Gaudain.

@

Under the sign of Aquarius, the eleventh house of the astro-logical chart deals with the ability to make friends and to handle non-emotional relationships, like those with teach-ers and counsellors, masters and protectors, and colleagues within associations or social groups. It's also the house of wishes and desires, of life's expectations and goals. It's the house of generosity and solidarity, of great humanist visions, of ideals and projects. Under its influence, we find mutual support, the protection of partners sharing common ideas and helping each other establish roots in society. The eleventh house is the house of experience and responsibil-ity, of working to improve society. It's the house of sharp wit, humour, and popularity. It's also the house in which we gain our independence by refusing limitations.

@

I'd known who Camil Gaudain was for a long time — people who alter the common spelling of their names tend to draw some attention. But, although we'd said hello from time to time, this was really the first time we'd ever spoken to each other. He offered a pleasant smile:

"I hear your next book is coming out with Gallimard? . . . Hot stuff . . ."

Now there was a wild notion if ever I'd heard one, although I confess I found it amusing. I took my time to savour each syllable before correcting him. "Nice rumour. And where did it come from?"

"I heard it on CJSE yesterday, round suppertime."

Well, that beat all! Some literary fanatic had taken over the airwaves of the community radio station. It was too perfect. I was in no hurry to burst the bubble. Maybe I needed a bit of just this sort of fantasy, a kind we don't get too much of in these parts. I tried to drag the thing out a bit without seeming to. "My next book isn't even written, I can't imagine how Gallimard could be interested in publishing it."

"All it takes is a good agent. They also said you were going on French television in the fall."

News sure travels fast. I was launched. *Bouillon de culture* had staked its claim to me. Worst of all, they had me crossing oceans while I was still struggling just to get out of town.

☙

Over time, the impression Terry had formed of Carmen during the excursion on the *Beausoleil-Broussard* softened. Far from always asking questions, Carmen turned out to be a quiet young woman. Although, like anyone who's lived by the sea, she showed great single-mindedness.

"What do you know about the Bouches-du-Rhône region?"

Terry thought for a second. "If it's what I think, my uncle's got some in his cellar."

Carmen couldn't help laughing. "And who might your uncle be?"

"Alphonse Thibodeau."

"The cabinet minister?"

"Uh-huh."

". . ."

". . ."

"And what's he minister of, again?"

"Culture."

". . ."

". . ."

"Bouches-du-Rhône is a delta in France. Ever seen a delta?"

"You sure got a thing for deltas, eh?"

". . ."

". . ."

"You ever seen a delta?"

"Nope."

". . ."

"There's the Mississippi, too."

"I know."

@

Listening to Camil Gaudain it occurred to me that he couldn't have read my books. What's more, I was afraid he was getting the wrong idea, that he imagined they were better than they really were.

"No, I'd be mighty surprised if Gallimard was interested in my books."

"Why? Your books are good!"

He seemed so sincere that it warmed my heart. But I stopped playing along, for fear of ruining it. Everything was happening too fast; I decided to set things straight right away. "To be perfectly honest, I'm not exactly overjoyed about this trip to France. I don't tell this to everyone, but, well, I'm agoraphobic."

Camil Gaudain seemed to understand. He lay his hand on my shoulder and said, laughingly and without really lowering his voice, "Don't worry about it, I've got AIDS."

◎

And what would I say on *Bouillon de culture*? That death, or at least nonexistence, is inscribed in our genes? That everything depends on the way, the art, of accepting this? That everything's a matter of legitimization? Legitimizing what we are in the eyes of the world and in our own eyes. To appear to be, to be to appear. To see and to be seen. Recognized. That not everything depends entirely on chance, on the invisible and the unfair. To retrace the course of history, to descend into the unconscious in search of causes, explanations, justifications, interpretations of one's own existence in places where there is sometimes no other way to be, to exist, to see and be seen, recognized. And finally, perhaps yes, for all these reasons, to write.

XVI

THE TERRE-ROUGE CAFÉ was one of a number of businesses that had sprung up since the creation of the Petitcodiac park. In good weather the café opened its terrace, next to an ancient little cemetery. Terry and Carmen often sat there.

"Back when they were building the city, they found coffins made of three-inch boards in there. That's how they knew it was an Acadian cemetery instead of an Indian one."

"On account of the three inches?"

"Uh-huh."

Across the way was one of the city's most pleasant neighbourhoods. A group of Acadian women had established a very pretty housing cooperative, the Coopérative du Coude, where those with a taste for gardening had access to small parcels of good land to grow flowers and vegetables.

@

Under the sign of Virgo is the sixth astrological house, the house of harvests, of accumulations and reserves. It's also the house of discernment, resourcefulness, and efficiency. The house of the primacy of mind over matter, it is where the struggle between consciousness and materiality occurs, where animality cedes a little to questioning. It's the house of habits, including emotional habits; the house of order, of perfectionism, and of fine tuning. Here too, we find clothing and structure, techniques and abilities. The sixth house is also the house of thankless or imposed labour: the house of service and hard work, dependants and pets, pensioners and handicapped people. It's the house of the stress caused by time and of the tendency to want to do too much. For those in this house, life can get dull if they don't introduce some magic.

Though he was extremely happy with his new condition, Hans was in no hurry to turn things upside down. He wanted to be sure he was not labouring under an illusion. For a while, he was content to see the world with new eyes, and that was enough. He was happy to see that the novelty didn't wear off; the illusion, if it was an illusion, was not fading. The more time passed, the more what might have been an illusion strengthened, was confirmed, and became rooted in reality. Reality itself took on a new form. It became the only possible reality, the only one that truly allowed him to advance, to take a step. The step.

And so, Hans began to rid himself of his possessions. All his possessions. He did this with care, striving to get a fair price for each object, but without digging in when demand resisted supply. Bit by bit, he put the money he made into a bank account, accumulating it until the day came when everything was sold, until the day when he was left with only the essentials. On that day, he returned to the diamond merchant and bought twelve stones, choosing them one by one, in spite of their marked resemblance. He opted for a size that could be resold easily. That same evening, he made a little cloth pouch that would contain them and that, from that day forward, he would wear against his chest.

That day, Terry and Carmen dallied longer than usual in the Terre-Rouge neighbourhood. They walked along Cran Street and de la Brosse, up to the small square where workers were erecting a monument to the first colonists of the Coude. Carmen read the historical plaque.

"Are these your folks, then, the Thibaudots?"

"Looks like it."

Carmen was impressed.

Which embarrassed Terry. "Well, we weren't entirely alone. There were the Babinots and Breaus too, in the beginning. And nearby, up to Memramcook on that side and Salisbury on this side, there were Blanchards, Gaudets, Broussards — starting with the father of Beausoleil — Melansons, Surettes, LeBlancs, Doucets, Saulniers, Landrys, Légers . . ."

"You learn all this by heart?"

"Had to, for my job."

Carmen continued to read the plaque. "Well, all the same, says here you were the first, around 1700."

"That was more around Memramcook really."

Although the monument to the Thibaudots, Breaus, and Babinots, the first colonists of Terre-Rouge, was already on its pedestal, it was still under a cloth. Workers were putting the finishing touches to the landscaping. Terry Thibodeau bent at the foot of the monument and grabbed a handful of earth. "The earth was actually supposed to be redder around here. That's why they called it Terre-Rouge. Some folks say there was another river, the Scoudouc, joined up with the Petitcodiac somewhere around here and that was the river that brought the red earth over all the way from Prince Edward Island."

This book, which wanted to be simple and as organic as a handful of earth, wavers now between a handful of earth and a handful of diamonds. Between the passage of time in which we take root and the passage of time in which we become petrified. Encrusted. In which we descend into layers of matter. To become forever immobilized. Mineralized. From slow, cultivated emotion to violent, fossilized emotion. Wavering between the realms of genealogy and geology. Between carbon paper and carbon, layer upon layer of time. The diamond being, after all, nothing more than carbon compressed over millions of years.

Carmen and Terry were strolling through the pretty streets of the Coopérative du Coude. They went up des Saules Street, turned on Toises, and walked up to what was once King Street but had been renamed Rue Royale.

"Some folks say a river with big tides like the Petitcodiac divides folks. That, most times, those who live on one side or the other of a river have a lot in common, but actually it's the other way around when tides are big. Folks get separated instead of brought together." Terry had become talkative, almost long-winded. Carmen wondered if he hadn't begun to enjoy having an audience. "'Cause there was trouble right from the start, among the French themselves. They fought over the best land. Even before the Expulsion, even before the Triteses, the Lutzes, the Joneses, the Steeveses, the Somerses, and the Wortmans arrived on Captain Hall's sloop in 1766."

XVII

THE MORE TIME PASSED, the more urgent it became to solve my problem. One possible solution kept coming back to mind. I picked up the telephone.

"Camil Gaudain?"

"In person."

"It's France Daigle . . ."

"Well, hello there! How are you?"

"Not too bad. I'd like to talk to you about something, have you got five minutes?"

"Sure."

"Good, well, I won't beat around the bush. And don't be shy about saying no if —"

"Don't you worry, no one ever accused me of being the shy type."

"Good, well, I was wondering if you wouldn't mind coming along with me to France so I can go on that *Bouillon de culture* show?"

Short silence on the other end of the line. My proposal seemed to have caught him by surprise.

"My gosh, I'm flattered, but . . . can't your friend go?"

"Well, she did want to go, but she can't get time off just then."

"Lord! And what kind of so-and-so does she work for!"

It was the only hesitation. Camil Gaudain agreed to accompany me and, to judge from the rest of the conversation, we were going to get along just fine.

❦

That morning, Élizabeth was truly happy lounging in the arms of Hans. She felt as though she would never have to hurry again, that nothing would ever be as charming and sweet as this moment of doing nothing but being. Even Hans's questions bothered her little. Their exchanges had become a kind of game, pleasant and enlightening in a way and without consequence.

". . . but you're a doctor."

"One has to do something. To keep busy. Stay interested."

"Just that?"

"That's already quite a lot."

"What about passion? Desire? Will?"

"You mean hope, the ideal, the grandeur?"

"Yes, all of those."

". . ."

"No?"

"I don't know. The more I go on, the more doubts I have. And, at the same time, the more I doubt, the more I go on."

❦

As usual with Terry and Carmen, the day's topic resurfaced at night.

"And what about you? Is there no one famous in your family?"

Carmen pretended to think about it before replying. "My father was named businessman of the year seven times in Kent County."

"Really? What does he do?"

Carmen had a pretty good idea of the effect her answer would have. "Diamond Billiards mean anything to you?"

In disbelief, Terry sat right up in bed. Arthur Després was a local millionaire whom everyone respected, mainly because he didn't appear to have stepped on anyone on his way up the ladder of success. "He's your father? And how is it you never thought to tell me?"

"Don't know. I guess it never came up."

Hans was intrigued by Élizabeth's attitude. He couldn't quite grasp her point of view, what the source of her freedom, her detachment, was exactly. "But you'll go back to it?"

"Of course."

"When?"

"I don't know."

"They're not expecting you?"

"Yes and no."

"But don't they depend on you?"

"They're waiting. They know. And someone's replacing me in the meantime. There are lots of doctors now, you know. We can relieve each other."

But Hans, being European, wasn't used to the wide open spaces of the North American mind. He was lost in this sort of vagueness. "You say they know. But what is it they know?"

"They're Acadians. They know nothing is black and white."

"Arcadians?"

"A-cadians. Without the *r*. They're the folks who live there. Of French descent. It goes back to the time of the discovery of America. A long story."

"And these A-cadians, they're in no hurry?"

"Let's say they have an instinct for detachment. It's a kind of sixth sense."

One subject led to another. Fame, Carmen's father, billiards, and the lousy music they play in pool halls exhausted themselves, but the subject of music remained in the air.

"Did you see Bob Dylan when he came to Moncton?"

The question amused Terry. "Well, sure! What do you think!"

"Did he sing 'Tangled up in Blue'?"

"No."

". . ."

"Well, he couldn't sing 'em all, now could he!"

"I suppose not."

"And you, where were you?"

"Toronto."

"You never told me that. And what were you doing there?"

"Good question."

I spoke to Camil Gaudain a few times on the phone before our departure, mainly about buying plane tickets and other such details. I also wanted to know, without saying so, if he felt physically able to make the trip, if there was any danger of him falling suddenly ill.

"My dear, as far as I can tell, my internal mix is stable. No matter how many ways I look at it, I can't see how a one-week trip to Paris could do anybody any sort of harm unless we run into terrorists."

Neither Camil nor I saw any need to see each other before leaving. We'd have plenty of time to get to know one another during the trip. And so, we ended our last phone conversation in good spirits with his words, "It's often best not to know too much in advance."

XVIII

AT FIRST, ÉLIZABETH looked without understanding at the small pile of diamonds Hans had removed from his pouch. She saw the diamonds there, pell-mell, shining, and free, and no thought came to her. There was nothing to conclude. She thought of touching them, picking them up, and letting them fall like sand, and then she did. And she liked the idea, the idea of a small pile of diamonds one carries around, casually, without showing them. For the diamonds could have been arranged, set in order one next to the other, fixed for all time on a necklace, a brooch, a ring. But that way, one would always see the same facets. Inlaid in the general surface of the world, in all the beauty and wealth made to be exhibited and admired, they would be deprived of the freedom to show themselves from all angles.

◎

Under the sign of Pisces, the twelfth house of the astrological chart is the house of all things hidden. This is the house of the mystery within oneself, of secrets, but also of regrets and unacknowledged, unconscious, or forgotten remorse. It's the house of all that we conceal, which includes weaknesses, limitations, sorrows, and handicaps without excluding strengths. It's the house of the private or reclusive life, of confinement, imprisonment, and illness. It's the house of endings and, in that capacity, it includes hospitals, prisons, and asylums. It's the house of self-destructive action and dependency, of undiagnosed diseases and accidents. It's the house of fatality, exile, and solitude; the house of criminality, obstacles, and life's material difficulties. In short, it's the house of the human condition with all it entails in the way of philosophical death, the struggle for inner healing, and contemplation. In this house, we abandon some of our rigidity, including the rigidity of the body, for a future that has become desirable. It is in the twelfth house that we attempt to judge ourselves objectively, that we listen once more to the collective unconscious, and that we undertake the pilgrimage of dissolution.

@

And then Élizabeth felt like laughing. By their very presence, the little stones banished seriousness from every situation. Better still, the presence of these little diamonds capsized everything into the pleasure of the unknowable. Something marvellous made Élizabeth not want to know. She enjoyed floating in the absence of genesis. In any case, she knew that everything was both good and bad. There was nothing to be suspicious about and she suspected nothing. She found herself face to face with pure wealth.

Troubled by her silence, Hans sought to reassure her. "They're mine. I —" But he stopped talking when Élizabeth lay her finger gently on his lips to silence him. They remained cross-legged, face to face on the unmade bed, with the little pile of diamonds lying on the rumpled sheets between them. And in the silence, in their eyes, in their internal and external laughter, desire surged once more within them.

☉

Camil Gaudain expressed only one concrete wish regarding the trip to Paris. "What would you say to a visit to the Place de l'Étoile?"

"You mean going up the Arc de Triomphe?"

"Yes. I'd really like that, to look down the length of the grand avenues, the twelve points. I've always wondered if the Place de l'Étoile was fashioned in the style of the old cities, like Rome for example. In those days they really knew ritual. You had to learn how to found a city. They even taught it. Not like today. Back then they didn't do it in any which way."

☉

There was no longer any possibility of concealing daylight in the room in which Hans and Élizabeth lay entangled in the silence of love. This room somewhere in Greece had once again become simultaneously anyplace and the centre of the world. The three axes extended in the six directions, as they should, and all the numbers were in alignment, as they had been since the beginning of time. They had squared the circle. And since nothing could be opened further, they had to begin again.

"Aren't you afraid of losing them or being robbed?"

Hans didn't know what to say. He had been afraid someone might suspect him of stealing them. But the possibility that someone could steal them from him had never occurred to him. No more than the possibility of losing them.

@

That night, as she watched Terry take out a condom, Carmen said, "Never mind that thing, we don't need it."

Terry didn't understand. The results of his tests hadn't come back yet, nor had hers for that matter. Carmen insisted. "I know you don't have AIDS, and I don't either." Terry didn't know what to do. Until Carmen shouted from the bathroom, "Okay, put it on then, if you like, but make a little hole in it so I can get pregnant."

4

In a Less than Perfect World

IXX

SINCE THE START of the school year, Terry's passengers on the *Beausoleil-Broussard* had been mostly students. Everything had been done so that the young people, who showed up at the park excited and jumpy, would emerge from the excursion calm and edified. Which demonstrates how carefully prepared the park guides' presentations had to be.

"You like it with the kids?"

"Well, there's some that stick their nose in everywhere. There was a girl today started to unscrew the name of the boat."

"A girl?"

"There's no difference anymore. Girl, boy . . ."

"Usually, they just paint the name on . . . it's not something you can take apart."

"I know."

". . ."

". . ."

". . ."

"Just the same, there's some that say kids are smarter nowadays."

❀

In spite of what she'd said to Hans — not that there wasn't some truth to her words — Élizabeth knew very well that this trip, which she'd undertaken on a whim, or almost, would have to end. She did have some room to manoeuvre but it couldn't last forever. And though she'd enjoyed her unfettered wanderings, she wasn't too unhappy to end them. It was her relationship with Hans that perplexed her. Did she want to end it as well, or was there something to prolong? She told herself that the pleasure of their relationship was linked to the fact that they had found each other at a time when they were both free, like dropouts, at an identical moment in their lives. She wasn't certain that there should be something more. The truth was that she wasn't sure she wanted more. Did this mean she wasn't really in love with Hans? And yet, she liked him so very much, and she loved to love him.

❀

Terry took other groups on excursions. Sometimes they were business colleagues on a group excursion or convention-goers gathered in Moncton. The tourist season ended in mid-October. Terry would work an additional week storing the equipment. Then he'd look for a winter job or collect employment insurance until the following season. The prospect of a winter without work didn't frighten him. He was used to downtime and, besides, now there was Carmen. She was the first true love of his life.

"I like your apartment. Fact is, I like it a whole lot better than mine. There's more to look at outside."

"All the same, yours is bigger. I'd like it if mine was as big as yours."

"Looks plenty big enough to me."

"Don't know. Feels too small. There's times I thrash about in circles and don't know what to do with myself."

"Well, those times, why don't you just come over to my place?"

"And what is it you think I do, then?"

◎

Élizabeth told herself that perhaps she had mostly loved being loved. It was as though she had discovered the comfort love brings. Or simply comfort itself. She couldn't be sure Hans was the main source of this feeling of comfort. It might already have been within her and she was only now discovering it. Or perhaps she had always known it was within her but she'd never known quite how to channel it or what to do with it. She suspected that deep down she'd never thought it important. At some point, she must have decided comfort wasn't something you could live on. That a sense of well-being was not legitimate. You needed more, to do more. Recently, this feeling of comfort seemed always near at hand, glued to her skin, the same skin Hans had tenderly brushed up against, refreshed, rekindled, awakened, and rocked to sleep. Now she carried all this within her. She was conscious of it. And it brought her a kind of peace.

◎

A few weeks before the end of the season, Terry learned that he would be receiving a group of important dignitaries aboard the *Beausoleil-Broussard*: a delegation responsible for the organization of the Francophone Summit in Moncton the following year. The upscale excursion was

planned for Friday, October 16. Normally, tours on the
Petitcodiac were terminated several days before then, but
the arrival of dignitaries constituted a sufficiently exceptional circumstance to prolong the season slightly.

"They just want to have an idea what it is. Could be
they'll make it part of the official program. Imagine that, eh,
all those folks on the Petitcodiac?"

"Won't work."

"On account of?"

"They won't have time. Too much to do. They always
make a big fuss over that sort of meeting, then sometimes it
lasts hardly two days."

". . ."

". . ."

"Well, even so, you never know."

". . ."

". . ."

". . ."

"If the river tides are just right . . . it might fit with their
schedule."

☺

Of course, I had to go over and tell Marie how things were
working out. This time she was busy putting things away,
but she'd just put a *rapûre*, a variation of Acadian poutines,
in the oven. "We were down to the Bay last weekend, so I
brought some back. You're staying for dinner, I hope."
Marie had married a Surette from Grosses Coques. As the
eldest in a large family, he returned to Nova Scotia often on
important family occasions. "And when is it you're leaving,
then?"

"In exactly twelve days, the fourteenth. A Wednesday.
You won't guess who with!"

Marie's eyes were sparkling. I hadn't really intended to
make her guess.

"With Camil Gaudain."

"Camil Gaudain! Now, there's a good idea!"

"I don't even know him, really. It just happened that
way, we met and got to talking. One thing led to another
and I asked him to come along."

"He's the perfect fellow! They don't come any nicer. You
see, everything's worked out fine. I just knew it would."

I've said it before: Marie's confidence is boundless. It's
beyond even her. "You're lucky to be able to see things the
way you do."

"That's my luck. Others have got something different.
You write."

"I suppose so."

Marie bristled. "And what do you mean, 'I suppose so'?
They're bringing you all the way to Paris to talk on TV! What
more do you want?"

I had to admit she was right. "You're right."

"Darling, you're going to go far in life, whether you like
it or not." And with those words, she reached up to grab a
tiny flask stored on top of a cupboard. "Here. It's lavender
oil. They say it relaxes you on the airplane. Smells good,
too. Look." She opened the small bottle, held it under my
nose. The scent of lavender filled my nostrils, masking for a
few precious seconds the delicious odour of *rapûre* that
had begun to fill the kitchen.

XX

TERRY DIDN'T DARE admit it to himself but the excursion with the French dignitaries was weighing heavily on his mind. Carmen sensed his nervousness.

"Here, read this, why don't you."

Terry took the books. They were two Astérix hard-cover comic books. He opened one. "And you think I'll be able to understand it?"

Carmen reached into her pocket. "Oh, and I found this as well."

Terry extended a hand. "My medal! I never even noticed I'd lost it."

@

For several days now, Hans has known that Élizabeth's departure is imminent. He's always known they would part but he's tried not to think too much about it. Now, rather than sadness, he feels amazement at the perfection that has led him here, to this room, and into the presence of this admirable woman to whom, when all things are considered, he doesn't want to become attached. This perfection manifests itself each time he removes a piece of clothing from the cupboard to fold and place in his suitcase. Perfection is concealed in the order and logic of the gesture, in the idea that envelops first the gesture, then the object: his folded woollen sweater, his two undershirts. Hans finds comfort in the act, in the clothes (his woollen socks, his two pairs of pants — one thick cotton, the other corduroy — his T-shirts, and his polo shirts), in the pockets of his suitcase, in his Swiss Army knife and its corkscrew, in his next destination, nebulous or unknown though it may be. And then there's his jacket, which he chose so carefully and which he keeps always close at hand, his jacket which, like a suit of armour, pulls him together and protects him from the world.

I'd been preparing my bags for Paris for some time. I jotted down items I wanted to bring as they occurred to me. I was especially afraid of forgetting any of the comforting things that might help me in the event of a panic attack on the plane: Walkman and various tapes selected to counterbalance every case of nerves, including a relaxation tape; homeopathic pills; jewellery and other copper knickknacks intended to ground me; a short book about letting go; a bottle of water and something small and healthy to snack on, although the presence of food in my bags can have a perverse effect and induce panic rather than mollify it; tranquilizers, just in case; two paperbacks and a magazine, so that I could at least appear normal; chewing gum, mainly to offer to others; a Game Boy; paper and pens, just in case writing might save me, yet again. All this in one of the big soft-leather bags with multiple compartments I'd purchased to blend in with the crowd, feel fashionable, and ensure a high degree of self-organization. All the same, I couldn't

forget the enormity of my camouflage: I could already picture the day when I would deliver myself to the airport,
decked out in this disguise of normality which was almost
as heavy to carry physically as it was mentally. In spite of
myself, I was afraid I'd be unable to board the plane as a
complete person or, even better, as a writer whose talent
and pertinence had at last been recognized. Instead, I saw
myself climbing on with the distinct impression of being
nothing more than a walking first-aid kit, a jumble of stop-
gap solutions.

⊚

Remote control in hand, Terry spent longer and longer
intervals watching the images of TV5 flicker by. One night,
they ran a report on France's rivers.

"Just the same, their rivers sure got weird names. The
Somme, the Meuse, the Garonne, the Loire . . . you'd think
they were talking in a different French language." And
indeed, once they were out of his mouth, the names went
nowhere; they remained suspended in the air, unburdened
by any gravity, reality, materiality, image, or preconceived
idea.

"I know what you mean. It's as though we weren't made
to open our mouths that way."

"Loire. The Loire . . ."

"Well, it's not as different as all that. It's like the word
gloire."

"Well sure, but that's not a word we hear too often round
here, now is it."

⊚

Élizabeth and Hans parted company at the Tel Aviv airport. After Greece, they had travelled here and there, and eventually found themselves on the banks of the Jordan River. Hans was still carrying against his chest the pouch containing the twelve small diamonds, invisible even to the airport metal detectors. Élizabeth had maintained within and around her the sensation of comfort, the impression of no longer being entirely a stranger. A stranger to what? To others? To herself? To the world as a whole? All of the above. Although she was about to leave Hans, she wasn't really leaving him. Perhaps they would meet again. Their paths might cross sooner or later. There was no hurry. This feeling of having rediscovered time was also part of Élizabeth's comfort: time had become a positive thing.

For Hans too, life would go on. Meeting Élizabeth had been a joyous thing, but it had been entirely unexpected. He had watched Élizabeth for a long time, sitting in the terrace of that small restaurant in Corfu before approaching her table and speaking to her. He hadn't come this far, psychologically speaking — the Netherlands wasn't that great a distance from the Mediterranean — to drop everything at the sight of a beautiful woman, no matter how exceptional she was. Hans was looking neither for *a* woman nor for *the* woman. In fact, he wasn't looking for anything in particular. His divestment and his departure lay before him like a long road to something he couldn't know and which, for that very reason, was impossible to seek out. But if he wasn't looking for a woman, what then did his encounter with Élizabeth signify? A test? A trial? A trap? A false start? None of these resonated in any way with Hans. It seemed to him, rather, that this meeting with Élizabeth had been a meeting with himself, a meeting of Hans with Hans made possible through acts of tenderness, beauty, and intelligence, through the soul within the body and the other in oneself. That explains why he had watched Élizabeth for so long at that small table on the terrace before approaching her, in order to love her for herself before loving her for himself.

◎

Before I passed the first point of no return, where security agents X-rayed the contents of my bag, Camil Gaudain suggested in a light and friendly way that I let go and enjoy the trip. He couldn't know how much I felt like a Christmas tree loaded down with more or less reliable lights, uncertain whether they would glow . . . or explode.

"You okay?"

"Just fine."

XXI

I EXPECTED TO FEEL the first paradoxical effect of my agoraphobia just after takeoff, in full flight, when all possibility of retreat would be cut off. It's always at such times that I'm overcome and submerged by a wave of unpleasant thoughts and sensations, a wave I fear will be fatal. This engulfing invasion has always abated, but not without leaving me shaken, weakened, vulnerable. And so, feverish and confused, clinging to everything and nothing, I am obliged to see life in all its facets, which, I suppose, is not such a bad thing.

Camil Gaudain didn't try to distract me in some superficial way from my temporary insanity. He understood perfectly his role as a life preserver and floated discreetly by my side, ready to intervene should I show serious signs of drowning. He observed everything calmly, occasionally pointing out some curious detail. Some time after takeoff he became more talkative.

"You know, some years back when I was bored with my job, I registered for a night course at the university. I'd always been interested in the classics and, well, one thing led to another and, don't ask me why, I ended up reading Freud, Jung, and all those guys."

A male flight attendant passed and inquired, with a pleasant smile, if everything was all right. At that moment I could honestly say yes. I was even able to make a bit of conversation.

"I don't know if it's me, but I have the feeling that male attendants are always nicer, more sincerely attentive to passengers than female attendants are."

"Really?"

"The women seem to march down the aisle without really looking at us. As though, right at the start, they pick out their favourites, usually men, and put all their energy into pampering them through the flight."

For several minutes, we studied the behaviour of male and female flight attendants. Camil agreed with me.

"You know, I think you're right. The men seem to pay attention to everybody. I never noticed that before."

But I had no desire to be completely right. "Well, there's one woman over there who doesn't seem to discriminate. But she's the only one. Looks like the others don't want to see a thing."

@

Unable to sleep that night, Carmen sat up in bed and lit a cigarette. Terry lay a hand lazily on her thigh but he hadn't the slightest intention of doing more.

"What would you say, then, if we were to spend next winter over there?"

" . . ."

She knew Terry wasn't sleeping. "Eh? Well, what do you think?"

"And where might over there be?"

"Louisiana, or France."

" . . . "

"We can decide over a game of pool. If you win, we go to Louisiana; if I win, it's France."

At last Terry turned over, but slowly. Then he sat up, as though it were all very serious. "You mean the whole winter?"

"For as long as we can stand it. We could come back in the spring. Unless we stay longer. You never know, could be we won't want to come back."

Terry looked at Carmen's face. He tried to see if something so important could be decided in such a way. It looked to him like it could.

◎

Having spent his entire life by the sea, Camil too was single-minded. He took up the conversation exactly where the friendly flight attendant had distracted us.

"In any case, what I remember from Jung, primarily, is the sacrifice of intelligence. I've often thought about that idea, that it's our intelligence that impedes us. That we shouldn't expect to understand everything."

" . . . "

"I don't know why I'm telling you this."

I was mulling over the concept. "Would that be the same thing as holy indifference?"

Camil thought for a moment. "Seems like it might be something like that."

" . . . "

" . . . "

" . . . "

"I don't think Jung was a Catholic."

And after another brief pause, he added, "It's funny how I've always liked writers. I'm not saying that for your benefit. No, it's true. I find they're not like other folks. They always have something that doesn't work quite right and that's usually what brings them success." Then, "Well, if I really think about it, I can't honestly say I like them all. But it's as though I'm predisposed to liking them all." With those words, he burst out laughing and turned to face me squarely. "As you can see, there's a reason I got AIDS."

◎

Terry looked straight in front of him and thought about Carmen's proposal while she crushed ashes in the ashtray with her cigarette.

". . ."

". . ."

"There's just one thing."

"And what would that be?"

"If we go to France, you might have to change your name. Over there, they'll be calling you Thierry."

Terry burst out laughing, letting himself fall back onto the bed. Carmen loved to hear him laugh.

◎

In the end, the flight to Paris went very well. Camil's company had been very relaxing and I hadn't had to resort to my first-aid kit. I did, however, pull out the flask of lavender oil from my pocket, just to let Camil have a whiff.

"Marie Surette gave me that."

"Not Édée's Marie! She comes from down my way, in Bas-Cap-Pelé. A real tiger that woman!"

After the landing, Camil demonstrated an uncanny ease in the airport. He followed the flow of the crowd without thinking too much and led us quite naturally to where we were supposed to go. In the unending series of alleys and corridors, where I would normally have been on the edge of collapse, I advanced instead as though on a cushion of air, wrapped in the warm sensation of having survived the worst.

"Camil, thanks so much for coming along on this trip. I really appreciate it."

"My dear, don't mention it. It's a real pleasure for me, too."

We were moving down a glass-encased corridor when I saw a woman I recognized coming toward us.

"Isn't she from Moncton? That woman in the grey-brown coat?"

Camil snuck a look at her. "Are you sure?"

"I think she's a specialist at the hospital."

"A psychiatrist?"

"No, oncologist, I think."

"French?"

"Don't think so. But she could well be."

"Well, she's not too shabby."

As we passed her, Élizabeth turned her head in our direction and saw us looking at her. She smiled, though timidly.

A few steps farther, out of her sight, Camil added, "She probably doesn't know where we're from."

"Well, when it comes to that, there's times I'm not so sure I do either."

@

Terry didn't know what to think. He no longer even knew how to think. "I'm hungry."

Carmen was butting her cigarette.

"I've got everything it takes to make nachos."

"Even sour cream?"

"Even sour cream."

"Naturally soured or artificially?"

Now Terry could tell she was pulling his leg. "Well, do you want some or don't you?"

"Can you make me some without the jalapenos? I won't get a wink of sleep tonight if I eat those things."

"Sleep? And do you suppose I'll be sleeping now, with all the crazy ideas you're putting in my head?"

XXII

THE SUN WAS RISING, but the air was cool on the morning of the sixteenth when Terry arrived at the pier for the dignitaries' cruise. On the way, he'd congratulated himself for dressing more warmly than usual so that he wouldn't have to suffer the cold in addition to his fear of being intimidated.

The visitors arrived as planned at 9:30. Four gleaming rental cars deposited about fifteen more or less appropriately dressed dignitaries in the parking lot. There were two Frenchmen, one of whom was a writer, three Africans, four representatives of the RCMP, the mayors of Dieppe and Moncton, and a half-dozen government representatives, including two provincial ministers. Three of the group were women: two senior civil servants and a high-ranking police official. All together, about twenty people boarded the *Beausoleil-Broussard*, counting the historical and ecological guides chosen for the trip and the park director, who had no intention of missing this boat.

@

The day before the taping of *Bouillon de culture*, Camil and I wandered the streets of Paris, taking time to adjust to the accents and intonations while the French, who probably took us for American tourists, replied to us in English more often than we would have liked. When we were tired, we stopped in the cafés.

"It's mighty strange. You'd think they couldn't hear us."

"I know."

"Maybe, just before they hear us, they see us and something doesn't fit right in their heads."

"Are you thinking we look as bad as all that, then?"

"Don't know. Sometimes, it doesn't take much."

". . ."

". . ."

"Could be they don't hear anyone at all."

"Well, there is that."

⊚

Terry went through all the routine checks not once but five times before casting off and giving the *Beausoleil-Broussard* its head in the open water of Le Coude, at the foot of Terre-Rouge. The river was brimming over with water that day and allowed for a true aquatic excursion rather than a long muddy slide. The sun was shining and so before they reached Fox Creek, they had all stopped shivering. At this first stop in the tour, the guides gave a brilliant account of Acadia's past, present, and its future, all to the rhythm of the waves of settlement and unsettlement in the Petitcodiac marshes. Even Terry was swept up in the tale. As he piloted the *Beausoleil-Broussard* toward the second and last stop of the tour, the site of the aboiteau, Terry realized that seeing this familiar landscape through the eyes of foreign delegates enhanced his own understanding. For the first time, he felt pleased to have been selected to pilot the excursion.

A typical Acadian snack of front-door-garden soup, *rapûre*, and apple dumplings had been planned at the Clapet restaurant following the boat's passage through the giant aboiteau. At the gate, before the boat actually went inside the dike, the guides made their presentation on the ancient but efficient technique of draining marshes. After the presentation, as usual, the *Beausoleil-Broussard* waited for an artificial current to generate, and allow it to enter the aboiteau and rejoin its own history. Once inside the enormous wooden chamber covered in earth and hay, further explanations were offered regarding the very latest technology park engineers had designed to create the impressive reproduction.

☞

Once we were in the *Bouillon de culture* studios, things began to go very quickly for Camil and me. In the blink of an eye, I found myself under French television lights, as though I were in a dream full of illogical and surprising transitions. Finally, the famous TV host turned to me.

". . . this book in which you not only admit to being an agoraphobe, but you embrace the disease. Really!"

"Well, you know, as your own Professor Jean Delay put it so well, every nervous disease is a revolution."

"Is that right?"

"Yes, because on the evolutionary scale, on the biological scale, if you will, everything is a matter of adaptation. Everything develops in response to the environment, to the surroundings. The changes may be infinitely small and gradual but once they take root, they are there for a very long time. From the point of view of such an astounding biological rootedness, with all the innumerable layers of life of which we are the repositories, any failure to adjust, no matter how insignificant, represents a real movement of resistance. What's surprising and a source of joy is that we still have the strength and specificity to react. And these are the attributes we admire in revolutions: their strength and specificity." For a split second I was almost frightened. I hadn't expected to become inflamed so quickly. I was afraid of what would follow. And so, I suspect, was Bernard Pivot.

"Say, you people in Acadia have been reading more than Antonine Maillet!"

"That's right, we don't limit our reading to Antonine Maillet. But her work helps us a great deal in reading ourselves as a people. Not all revolutions are bloody. Some even go unnoticed. One day, just like that, we realize they've happened."

"But let's get back to your book and agoraphobia." At this point, Monsieur Pivot remarked that in France the disease, when it isn't associated with some neurovegetal disorder or other, is better known under different names, such as spasmophilia or chronic fatigue syndrome. "This fear of open spaces then, this need to be enclosed, wouldn't you prefer to be cured of the illness rather than cling to it and brandish it like some revolutionary banner?"

"It's difficult to ignore the fact that women are its primary victims. How can we accept that? I therefore advocate in favour of a democratization of agoraphobia. We must work to share this disease equally among men and women."

"You're a feminist?"

"How can anyone not be for the happiness of women, as well as that of men, children, the elderly . . ."

"But let's get back to my earlier question: wouldn't you prefer to be cured than to carry your revolutionary banner?"

"It's true that agoraphobia is anything but convenient. I even had trouble getting here to your program."

"Really? As bad as that?"

"Yes, the airplane, the corridors, the crowds, the leaning buildings . . ."

"Leaning buildings?"

"Yes, on some street corners. It's rather peculiar."

"But it can be cured . . ."

"Apparently, some people are cured."

At this point, Bernard Pivot did what I was hoping he would; he opened my book and read an excerpt. He selected the bit about Hercules and the birds on the shores of Lake Stymphalus. Then he asked me, "Are you implying here that Acadia destroys the traveller?"

"One would have to be ignorant of Acadian history to claim Acadians are not travellers. Although in my case, it may be true. But even if the traveller is dead, the voyage continues."

This made Bernard Pivot laugh. I like to hear Bernard Pivot laugh. Then he picked up my book again, opening it this time to page 102. "What about this feeling of detachment, this Acadian sixth sense? You don't have it either?"

"No, not much anymore. I'm more likely to go the way of page 97. A fossil."

"Don't you mean a monument? Like that granite cube?"

Now I was the one to laugh. And to be taken by surprise. "Ooh la la! Lacan! Somebody! Help!"

@

More than once the Petitcodiac had demonstrated that it wasn't always willing to be harnessed, and so it wasn't surprising that something would go wrong that day. The real and artificial currents collided with full force and, when the sluice gate couldn't reopen, the *Beausoleil-Broussard*, which was supposed to remain enclosed within the giant aboiteau for no more than ten minutes, was stuck there for close to an hour. First there was general consternation but this was soon followed by astonishment that such a problem had never happened before. It was only when the dignitaries realized that their cellphones had ceased to function that the situation became truly serious.

Terry could communicate with technicians on land by marine radio and tried with them to find a way to extricate the little band of futurists from this historic mess. He followed their instructions, went through a series of basic checks, but, in the end, there was nothing to be done. They would simply have to exercise patience and wait for the currents to stabilize and the complex mechanisms to return to their normal operations.

Terry had just settled in and set himself to exercise patience when the writer in the French delegation stepped into the cabin. He entered without a word and began to look through the small aperture that afforded a glimpse of the light and the fields beyond the dam.

"I've got no vein."

Slightly taken aback and unsure of the meaning of the French expression, Terry didn't risk a response but cast a furtive glance at the Frenchman's wrists just in case.

"It doesn't wear you out?"

Terry hesitated. "You mean, am I tired?"

The Frenchman thought Terry had simply misheard his question. "It doesn't bother you . . . to be stuck like this, locked in?"

Terry fumbled for a simple answer. "No. I must be used to it."

"I hate it. It gives me the balls."

Terry tried to imagine what having the balls could mean. Nor did he have any idea what size of balls to imagine. He thought simultaneously of mothballs and of billiard balls. As the man stood there beside him in silence, Terry began to feel some kinship with him and wanted to lend him some encouragement. "Shouldn't be too long, I figure. They've found the problem."

"..."

"..."

"You mind if I haul one?"

Terry saw the pack of cigarettes in the delegate's hand and understood. Almost no one had the right to smoke in public anymore in Canada, but Terry didn't have the heart to break it to this pale and drawn man clearly in need of some air. Instead, he stepped forward, opened a small side window and closed another behind him. "Try to blow your smoke over that way."

The man offered him one but Terry wouldn't allow himself such a breach of conduct with the park director on board.

"..."

"..."

"All the same, Canada is a beautiful country. All those wide open spaces."

"Yeah. Most people like it."

"..."

"Well, to tell the truth, there's times I find it all too big really. It never ends."

"..."

"..."

"I'm sorry, I didn't catch your name."

"Terry."

"Thierry?"

"Terry. Terrence. Terrence Thibodeau."

"Terrence Thibodeau. Is that a typical Acadian name?"

"Hard to tell. I guess so."

The words were pouring out of my mouth as though they'd been dying to get out. From the corner of my eye, I could see Camil in the audience. I couldn't quite read his look of astonishment: should I restrain myself or press on?

Bernard Pivot was quick to take up the challenge. "In this book, you also deal with the difficult and confusing relations between Acadia and France . . . You describe an incident that takes place on the river . . . Hang on while I get the pronunciation of that name right." He leafed through *Just Fine* until he found the page. "Here it is . . . the Pe-tit-co-di-ac River. There's a delegation of officials on board a pontoon boat. Among them are some Frenchmen, including a writer. And only the writer takes the trouble to go up and speak to the young captain of the boat. Are you saying that only writers are sensitive to life and ordinary people around them?"

"Maybe. I suppose we have to try to maintain a myth or two. But you can't forget that this particular writer is anxious and that he approaches Terry, the commonest of mortals, precisely in the hope of clinging to some part of reality."

"Well alright, let's talk about young Terry, a very likeable character who wonders if one can survive without having read the Bible. But perhaps we should be talking instead about his uncle, Alphonse Thibodeau, the minister of culture who is also a lover of wine."

"Yes, we Acadians have taken a liking to wine."

"This minister, does he really exist, or is he a fictional character? Because, in your book — I don't know if this is a common style in your country — one can't easily distinguish the real from the fictional."

"Alphonse Thibodeau, minister of culture, is a fictional character."

"But you do have a minister of culture . . ."

"Hmm yes . . ."

"And what does he or she do exactly?"

"Oh, lots of things. They're responsible for municipalities and housing, for example."

"Oh? And who's responsible for language, for the arts?"

"Well, everyone I suppose, and no one."

"And this works?"

"You should come and judge for yourself."

"There's so much more we could discuss about this book, many metaphors and allusions that would be fascinating to explore, the painting by Bruegel the Elder, for example, and the Dieppe Landing with its tirade about heroism. And then there's the bit on the impact of tourism on ancient myths, like Sisyphus and the impossibility of leisure. And there are the symbols of the snail, the triangle, and the Trinity." Monsieur Pivot lifted his gaze from his notes and looked at me. I was afraid he was about to question me on the Trinity thing. Had I really written something about that? "And those sections on astrology . . . if I understand correctly, this book belongs under the influence of the twelfth house, which would be, in fact, the temptation of autobiography."

I found the remark extremely pertinent. "Indeed. I hadn't thought of it, but you're absolutely right."

"This autobiographical temptation is quite widespread today . . ."

"Yes. It's the wretched soul telling his or her story, as Raymond Carver describes it so well in 'Blackbird Pie.' For my part, I have to admit the autobiographical angle bothers me a bit. I would have preferred to avoid it, but I couldn't manage it. I don't know why, but I didn't want to hide, I couldn't hide the truth, the painful truth, in a fictional character, much as it embarrasses me to expose myself this way."

"One cannot escape one's time."

"True. I can't remember who it was that said artists don't have as much freedom as we'd like to think, that freedom is not absolute, that each era gets its share of freedom and even artists must be satisfied with that amount. I remember now: it was Kandinsky, I think."

XXIII

TERRY THOUGHT HE'D told Carmen the whole story of his half-hour with the anxious Frenchman in the helmsman's cabin of the boat. But, as days went by, he realized there were always bits left to tell. "He asked me what the Petitcodiac looks like in winter."

"What did you tell him?"

"Well, I had to think about it. Never had reason to describe it before. You don't often go describing something everybody can see for themselves."

"Well, what did you say, then?"

"I said the river doesn't freeze, though it does get filled up with snow and ice all around, and there's something like a big wall of earth and ice going up on either side. And while I was telling it to him, it came to me that that's the time the river's really and truly most beautiful. When it looks like nothing else, just water running along between two walls of earth and ice and sometimes a bit of mist floating just above."

"You think he could imagine it?"

"Well, I can't say, really. Probably not."

"   . . . "

"But, he did give me his card."

"His card?"

Terry took out the business card and gave it to Carmen. She studied it and handed it back. "Better keep it. You never know."

Terry took the card back and returned it to the little slot in his wallet from which he had taken it. "I wonder where Creuse might be."

☙

Camil had truly enjoyed watching the taping of *Bouillon de culture*. During the rest of our trip, he repeated several times how glad he was he'd agreed to come along with me. "And I really enjoyed listening to you. What you have to say is really interesting. I think you're brilliant. Seriously. I can't believe you really come from our parts."

"Well, to tell the truth, sometimes it would be a lot easier if I was just normal."

"Oh, we Acadians have trouble standing out. You'd think we were afraid of shining."

It was noon and hunger had begun to gnaw at us. We walked into an ordinary-looking café.

"I think I'll just have a hot dog in a baguette."

"Good idea. When in Paris . . ."

☙

After Élizabeth's departure, Hans wandered a while over the surface of the globe and the surface of things in general. He didn't actively seek out new destinations but was content to imagine contexts and atmospheres, climates and sonic backgrounds. He watched life unfold, allowing himself to be swept along and inspired by it. Worlds drifted through his mind. Some called out to him; others let him pass. Life without an ultimate goal seemed worthwhile in itself. There seemed to be value in the very lightness of life, as fragile as it was demanding in its equilibrium. He took the time to enjoy it without really analyzing it, without really attempting to describe it. He allowed himself to be penetrated by whatever sought to penetrate, he veered whenever called upon to veer, and he always ended up somewhere. When all was said and done — several days or several weeks later — he found he liked the fact that the world was round. Quite simply.

@

I was chewing on my merguez sausage and ruminating on our recent conversation. I felt bad about giving Camil the impression I wasn't proud of myself or happy with my lot in life. Of course, I enjoyed his compliments. But I kept remembering a discussion I'd had with the hairdresser who'd cut my hair a few weeks before the trip.

"You write books? Really? Geeeee . . . I had no idea anyone was doing that sort of thing round here."

"Oh yeah, there's a few."

"Really? Wowww . . ."

The incident made Camil laugh, although it must be said, he laughed easily. It was as though life was always tickling him. "Well, sure. It's true, sometimes the level does get pretty low. So low it crashes." He ordered two more glasses of wine, and added, "And why do you think I went and changed my name? Just to be different. But I'm not a good model for anyone, I should've gone a whole lot further." He raised his glass, tapped mine, and made his toast. "To Steppette!"

@

Then places began to spring up of their own accord. As though without cause. They passed rapidly through his mind, like a bolt of lightning over the landscape, without violating logic but suggesting the existence of other realities. Hans didn't want to focus his attention on these sudden apparitions. He was afraid they would disappear if he thought about them too much. He even tried not to wait for them. It seemed to him there was something blinding about waiting; it thrust him into another world and kept him from savouring this one. All this, and undoubtedly much more, put him on a plane to San Francisco. Even on board the plane, his destination seemed unreal, ethereal. It consisted of nothing more than a particular notion he had of light, of colour. In fact, it wasn't even an idea. It was more like a sensation, maybe even a scent or a breath. A breath of light and colour called to him. That was all he knew. But it was enough. It was even a lot.

☙

Camil and I were not given seats next to each other on the final leg of our journey, the flight from Montréal to Moncton. Everything had gone so well from the start that this seemed like only a minor setback. I found myself next to a woman from Painsec who was an employment insurance official returning from a training workshop in Ottawa. I sensed from one or two of her comments that she didn't enjoy travelling much and that these few days far from home had dragged on.

"There was a time, we travelled a lot. My husband was a trucker and we'd take off for two or three weeks at a time. We enjoyed it. We went everywhere, to Ontario, to the States. I've been pretty well all over the States."

"   . . ."

"Afterwards, when I couldn't go along anymore on account of the kids, he started taking them. One by one. Was pretty much the only way they'd get to see their dad."

"   . . ."

"Then we bought ourselves a house, and my husband opened a truck stop. The children're all grown up now. The eldest works with him."

"   . . ."

"I like it just fine at home. The youngest plays hockey. They're getting set to go play in some tournament in Switzerland. Makes me nervous. I can't imagine going. I can't imagine leaving these parts. Brrrr . . ."

XXIV

THE *Bouillon de culture* program I was on aired two weeks later in Canada on TV5. Which meant I was back home to receive comments on my performance. The day after the program, Marie told me that the phone had taken her away from her TV for a short time near the end of the program.

"It was my husband. I just about hung up on him. I don't figure I missed much."

By the time she'd got back to her seat, Bernard Pivot was wrapping up with his famous list of questions to guests. "And when you die, if God exists, what would you like to hear Him say to you, France Daigle?"

Being familiar with the list of questions, I'd had time to prepare my answer. "I'd like Him to say: 'For an agoraphobe, you managed fine. I kept a place for you near the door, so you can feel free to leave anytime, just in case.'"

And Bernard Pivot replied, "Because you think, even in Heaven, you might want to leave? It's true that when you were young, you were attracted by hell: the flames and that Satan's Choice biker, wait, I'm trying to remember his name . . . Chuque. Chuque Bernard. Did he really exist?"

"Yes, Chuck still lives in Dieppe. He's calmed down a bit over the years. Now he wears glasses just like yours."

❀

That evening, Carmen wore her little red dress and her brown leather top. She took longer than usual to get ready. She had amused herself posing in front of the bathroom mirror as though she were being photographed. She was giddy. More than that. She was happy.

When Terry appeared in the doorway, at the foot of the stairs, she saw that he too had made more of an effort to look good. He was freshly shaved and perfumed. His little luxury. She wouldn't make him wait. This was a big night and they were both up for the occasion.

They had chosen a pool hall a little out of the way where there was slim chance of meeting too many friends who would distract them from their game. They were, nonetheless, willing to be distracted a bit. It was part of the dynamic. Each one wanted to win — a matter of minor personal glory — but it was also crucial to be a good loser. Because, one way or the other, they would be going on a trip.

They selected everything that could be selected (the table, the lighting, the cues, the music in the jukebox, the ashtray, the drinks) and abandoned themselves to the rest, to all that they could never control and that they never wanted to control anyway.

Chalking up her cue, Carmen said, "There's just one more thing."

"What?"

"There'll be three of us."

" . . . "

" . . . "

Terry couldn't believe it. "You mean it worked! You're pregnant?"

"I never figured you'd dare."

He bent his elbow, clenched his fist, and pulled down on an imaginary lever with a solid, perfectly controlled Yeesss! Then he walked over to Carmen's side of the table, looked her in the eyes for a second before kissing her on the cheek, and asked, "Do you want to break?"

"No, you break. I'd rather you break."

Terry looked at the table, studied the balls in their pre-deltaic grouping, then turned and came back to Carmen. "We'll have to stop smoking, eh?"

"Yeah."

☞

Two or three days after the program aired in Acadia, Chuck Bernard picked up the phone.

"Hello?"

"Yes, I'd like to talk to France Daigle."

"That's me."

"France? This here's Chuck."

"Oh, well, hello!"

"France, can you believe it, the other night I'm zapping away and there you are. I guess it was in France. You were talking about your book. I just caught the tail end really. Then all of a sudden, would you believe, there's this guy who's saying my name . . . Chuque, Chuque Bernard, pronouncing it the fancy French way."

I had to laugh listening to him. "Yes, it was in Paris."

"You went to Paris to talk about your book?"

"Yes . . ."

"Well! That's great! I guess I'm gonna have to read it now. It made me curious-like. Where can a fellow buy a copy?"

"Well, I was going to bring you one."

"Oh, you're nice. You know what, I'm really proud of you."

"Well, thank you!"

"Oh, and while you're at it, can you bring me an extra copy? That way, I'll have one for home and one for the shop. You know what a show-off I am."

⊚

Camil Gaudain was a long way from death's door but he had to watch his health closely and undergo a battery of tests regularly. After his return from Paris, he was in the hospital for an examination when he saw Élizabeth in the snack bar on the ground floor. He was standing next to her, waiting to be served. "Did you have a nice trip?"

Élizabeth looked at Camil, a bit surprised.

"You don't know me. I went to Paris with a friend a few weeks ago — the writer France Daigle, you may have heard of her — and we saw you in the airport."

Now Élizabeth recognized him.

"You must have wondered what we were up to staring at you like that."

"No. Not really. I just wasn't sure I recognized you."

"I guess you see a lot of folks."

"I see quite a few, yes."

"Well, anyway, you look well."

Élizabeth was flattered by the compliment and she accepted it easily. "Thank you."

"You're not from Moncton . . ."

"I've been here for five years now."

This information stunned Camil to such an extent that he completely forgot his own situation. "Really! Just goes to show what you miss when you're not sick."

@

Hans is in no hurry to leave the San Francisco airport. Since he has all the time in the world, he makes an effort not to live too fast. He strolls by a few hallways looking at what the boutiques have to offer. He smiles at the window displays. There's something heartwarming, something human about life's objects presented this way. In one of the windows, he sees a puzzle of his compatriot Bruegel the Elder's *Census at Bethlehem*. In the past, he often and patiently contemplated this painting, and he lets himself look once again at the inhabitants crowding into the Green Crown Inn to pay their taxes to the emperor's men. He lingers over the contents of their baskets, their demijohns, and their crates of fowl, and the peasant slitting a pig's throat in plain view of everyone, his wife collecting the blood in a pan. He re-examines the people bent beneath their loads, walking across rivers frozen from shore to shore to join those who arrived some time ago and have arranged their barrel-shaped wagons filled with grain or wine in the square, and who are now discussing, negotiating, arguing, sharing news. He sees again the chickens in front of the inn pecking at the feet of the artisan who makes and sells his chairs, the three-legged straw seats parents use as sleds to pull their kids along the frozen river. He allows himself to be moved once more by the woman sweeping snow, the man lacing up his skates, the children spinning tops or tussling on the ice. He sees once again the crowd gathered around a fire and wonders if they're roasting wheat. He rediscovers the few people seated in the trunk of a not-quite-dead tree converted to receive the surplus of travellers. He hasn't forgotten that, here and there, people are pushing, pulling, taking care of business, building a cabin, carrying wood. In the courtyard of a small cottage, a peasant woman bends over her cabbages half-buried in the snow. There's also the dog, a few crows, and Joseph carrying a long saw on his shoulder, leading the donkey on which Mary, pregnant with Jesus, is seated. A bullock accompanies them as they prepare to replay the drama of Christianity in this sixteenth-century winter landscape.

Hans enters the shop, points to the puzzle, and buys it. Three thousand pieces. While the saleslady prepares the bill, Hans's gaze falls upon the child in his sleigh who propels himself forward with small poles he thrusts into the ice. He also sees again, in the centre of the painting, the abandoned wheel standing frozen in the snow and ice. It still has all of its twelve spokes.

"Thank you sir, and good luck. It's a big one."

"Thank you."

Hans leaves the shop and the airport with his suitcase in one hand and the puzzle in the other. He will make his way downtown and look for a room. There are only nine little diamonds left in the pouch on his chest.

Sometimes I feel the urge to take a trip. Alone. A trip for its own sake, for the sheer pleasure of travelling. And nothing more. It's an urge that comes often but never lasts long. In general, the urge never lasts long enough for me to make preparations, physically or mentally, especially mentally, to go. Recently, for example, I thought of London. I often think of London since I read Doris Lessing's collection of short stories *The Real Thing*. It's not a genre I care for but I truly enjoyed the atmosphere, what's said and left unsaid, everything surrounding English teatime. And I, whom subways turn to jelly, enjoyed touring London via the Underground with her. I enjoyed seeing through her eyes the many neighbourhoods we crisscrossed above ground. The book survived a recent housecleaning of our bookshelves. It's a book I'd like to read again if I don't take that trip, if ever I don't make it to London, or if ever I do.

18.99
MA